SEAL's Honor

AN ALPHA SEALS CORONADO NOVEL

Makenna Jameison

ISBN: 9798706528713

ALSO BY MAKENNA JAMEISON

ALPHA SEALS

SEAL the Deal
SEALED with a Kiss
A SEAL's Surrender
A SEAL's Seduction
The SEAL Next Door
Protected by a SEAL
Loved by a SEAL
Tempted by a SEAL
Married to a SEAL
Seduced by a SEAL
Rescued by a SEAL
Stranded with a SEAL
Summer with a SEAL
Kidnapped by a SEAL
SEAL Ever After

Table of Contents

Chapter 1

Jackson "K-Bar" Clinefield resisted the urge to groan as he pulled up to his teammate Raptor's townhouse. His buddy had planned a party for their SEAL team and dates that night so they could celebrate Blake "Raptor" Reynolds and his girlfriend Clarissa's engagement. She'd packed up her home in Texas, driven a few states over with his buddy, and moved in during the summer.

And now the two of them were living together, engaged, and happy as hell.

It had been a damn crazy few months, and seeing his friend content with a woman for maybe the first time ever wasn't a hardship. Jackson wasn't big on parties though, even less interested in relationships, and he knew the other guys would probably all be there with a woman.

Jackson would be the odd man out, not that he wasn't used to that. The younger guys on the team

1

had a new girl with them every week. Grayson "Ghost" Douglass had just gotten a serious girlfriend himself that he'd met in Bagram while on an op, and Troy never had a problem finding a lady friend for a night or two.

Jackson usually crashed and burned in actual relationships though—not that most of his friends were seriously seeing someone. But plenty of the beautiful women that he'd met over the years wanted the allure of being with a Navy SEAL, and those types were usually high maintenance and more trouble than they were worth. They might want to show them off to their friends or spend the night in their bed, but after that?

He just didn't have time for the drama.

He wasn't looking to be someone's meal ticket with his Navy career, and he wasn't looking for a woman who demanded he drop everything to cater to her every whim.

Jackson would be content with a normal woman— if they weren't so damn intimidated by his sheer size or risky career. The last woman he'd been with had broken it off when she couldn't handle his up and leaving abruptly for a deployment. Not that he had a choice in the matter.

He shut the door to his large black SUV and rounded the front, frowning when he spotted the woman next door hauling her trash to the curb. Most everyone in Raptor's neighborhood had those bins you rolled down, but hers seemed to be broken and missing a wheel. Her wavy dark hair hung down to her chest, and her tits looked fucking fantastic in the white tee shirt she wore.

Not that he'd noticed. Right.

Hell. She was the quintessential girl next door. Fresh-faced, toned, and somehow innocent as well. Maybe it was the white tee shirt and jeans. The women he and his teammates met at bars wore skimpy, sexy clothes. They were heavily made up and wanted male attention. This woman managed to be sexy as hell in a more natural way. Why she was hauling trash down to the curb instead of her boyfriend or husband was puzzling. Then again, there were lots of military guys in this town.

She could've been home taking care of everything while her man was overseas. There were plenty of military families in Blake's neighborhood.

"You need any help?" Jackson called out.

She jumped at his deep voice and looked over at him in surprise.

How she couldn't have noticed him standing there was beyond belief. At six-foot-five, he stood out everywhere he went. Then again, maybe she just wasn't paying close enough attention and had assumed he was Raptor. They both had dark hair and the builds of a SEAL, even though Jackson had a couple of inches on his friend.

He didn't like the way she trembled slightly as she looked at him though, or the slight hitch of her breath. "I won't hurt you," he said in a low voice, not moving a muscle. He nodded toward Blake's house. "I'm just here to see Raptor."

"Oh," she said, letting out a sigh of relief. "Right, you're one of his SEAL friends."

Jackson raised his eyebrows.

She shrugged, flushing slightly. "He didn't tell me; I just guessed. It's a Navy town, and he's always coming and going. Other men and women deploy for

3

a long time. He lives right next door, so of course I noticed when he'd suddenly be gone for a week or two."

She tugged on the trashcan again, and Jackson crossed the small yard to her, not liking to see her struggle. Maybe it was the chivalrous side of him—some women didn't appreciate it, but he'd been raised to treat a woman right. It wouldn't cause him any trouble to pull her trash to the curb, and he was a good foot taller than her. More even. He'd feel like an ass standing there watching her struggle.

And she seemed to know something about the military. His initial thought must've been right. She had a boyfriend that was deployed—he didn't see a wedding ring on her finger.

"I got it," he said gruffly. She looked surprised when he lifted up one side of the bin, holding the weight of it so he could pull it down the driveway on just the one wheel. "You should call and request a new can."

"I did, and they told me it was seventy dollars."

Jackson let out a low whistle. "That seems steep for a piece of plastic."

"Yeah, well, that's what I get for living in a safe neighborhood. Everything costs more. I'll just deal with it."

He nodded, looking at her from down by the curb. A weird feeling washed over him—there was just something right about looking at her standing there in the driveway. At his taking care of her. He'd never lived with a woman before, never had been married. This strange sense of déjà vu, like he'd always been taking care of her, felt right.

It was damn crazy, too, since he'd probably never

see her again. He usually saw his buddies on base or their local bar. They'd hit up the beach many a weekend afternoon. He rarely came over to Raptor's house, but damn. He'd clearly been missing out.

Hell if he couldn't see himself with someone like her though, which was strange. He didn't even know Raptor's neighbor and didn't do serious relationships since most women didn't like his unpredictable career. He'd been burned in the past when an ex had abruptly ended things, and the same scenario had repeated itself after that in one form or another.

Women liked the allure of dating a military man, but plenty of them just couldn't handle it. Raptor's own girlfriend, notwithstanding, they didn't like when he was sent out on ops and couldn't tell them where he was going or when he'd be home.

He'd always have secrets—that was simply the nature of his job.

Standing here wishing for something he couldn't have was damn crazy.

The woman's hair blew slightly in the breeze, and the sight of her brushing it back behind her ear made his chest hurt. She was just so damn innocent standing there.

He walked slowly back toward Raptor's house, trying to get his head on straight. He didn't really want to leave without at least finding out the woman's name, but she already seemed a little skittish of him. And besides—he wouldn't go after another man's woman. Of course she had someone. A beautiful thing like that? She'd be snatched up right away in this town.

A pickup truck pulled into Blake's small driveway, and he watched Ghost and Hailey get out, nodding at his friend.

"Are you guys having a party or something?" Blake's neighbor asked.

"Yep. Clarissa just moved here from Texas, and she and Blake got engaged, so we're having a little get-together. You should come over," he found himself saying.

"Oh, no, I couldn't," she stammered. "I wouldn't want to intrude."

"It'd be no intrusion," he assured her, his voice low.

Hailey squealed as Grayson helped her out of his truck and then kissed her, leaning her over backwards in his arms. Jackson glanced back to see his mystery woman blushing.

Why that intrigued him so the hell much he didn't know. She was different from most women he met when he went out with his friends. Probably because she wasn't the type of woman to meet men in bars. Hailey and Grayson were making out in the driveway like they didn't have an audience. Giggling once more after Grayson lifted her back up, the two began walking inside, calling out hello and Ghost casting a knowing glance as Jackson stood there with Blake's neighbor.

Jackson liked the quiet brunette though and thought she was a hell of a lot more attractive than the scantily clad women he met on the beach or in bars. He couldn't exactly stand out here all night though. He'd freak her out even more, and his friends would wonder what was up. "By the way, I'm Jackson."

She nodded, suddenly looking nervous. He wasn't sure why, but he didn't like the slight fear in her eyes.

"I'm Taryn," she said, looking like she didn't want to tell him. He had the weirdest sense that wasn't her real name, which was odd. She had no reason to give him a fake name. It's not like he was some random guy she'd met at a bar. She lived next door to Blake. He could easily get her name from him if he'd wanted.

It was the slight hesitation in how it came out though—she stumbled the tiniest bit.

He watched her for a beat, and she began to grow flustered. "Anyway, I should go," Taryn said. "You've got your party, and I've got, well, things to do."

Jackson nodded, already feeling regret as she turned and quickly walked toward her front door. His gaze briefly dropped to her ass. Her jeans were form-fitting and hugged her damn well. Perfectly. She was barefoot, too, he realized as his gaze lowered.

Too damn innocent for a man like him.

She'd blushed just watching Gray bend Hailey over backwards and kiss her in the driveway. Hell. He'd been with his fair share of women over the years. In his younger days, he'd had no problem spending a single night with a woman. No one he'd met recently had caught his interest the way Taryn had though. But she seemed young—much younger than his own thirty-one years.

He watched to make sure she got safely inside her house and then finally turned, walking toward the front door of Blake's place. Maybe he'd ask Blake about her later on he thought as he jogged up the front steps. Something about Taryn intrigued him. And he couldn't shake the idea that she seemed to be hiding something.

Jackson strode into Raptor's without bothering to

knock, looking at the group gathered around the living room and open kitchen. Clarissa was sitting in Blake's lap on the large sofa, giggling. Ethan "Everglades" Flannigan was telling both her and his date for the night a sanitized story about their most recent op. Troy "T-Rex" Harrison was in the corner of the kitchen, kissing the blonde woman he was there with. Grayson and Hailey were getting drinks, Grayson sneaking in another kiss.

Jackson shook his head but then nodded at Logan "Hurricane" Hudson, who was grabbing a beer from the fridge and seemed to be there alone as well.

"You don't have a date?" Jackson asked, quirking his brow as Logan walked over.

Logan lifted a shoulder. "Well, I probably could've invited the woman whose bed I woke up in, but she wasn't too happy when I split."

He couldn't help the snort that escaped him. "Sounds about right."

"Who was the chick?" Grayson asked, popping the cap off of his longneck as he strode over. He wrapped an arm around Hailey's waist, pulling her close. She was nearly a foot shorter than Ghost but fit against him perfectly. Exactly like how the woman next door would've fit against Jackson—not that he'd be finding out.

Jackson shrugged. "She lives next door. I think I scared her when I offered to help."

Ethan's date giggled as she heard their conversation. "All you guys are rather big and strong. Not that I have any complaints," she teased, running her fingernails over Ethan's bicep.

Jackson smirked. "I don't think Everglades has any complaints either."

"Hell no," Ethan said.

"We get Navy guys in the bar all the time," his date said. "I'm lucky Ethan asked me out instead of some other fella. Otherwise, look what I'd be missing out on."

"It was lucky we were in there," he joked. "Usually we hit up Salty Sunset, but we had to avoid Raptor's one-night-stand and ended up in your bar a few times instead."

Jackson's gaze shifted to Raptor and Clarissa.

"No worries," Ethan said with a laugh. "Clarissa heard all about her. Considering Raptor only has eyes for her now, I don't think it's an issue."

Raptor muttered a curse. "We're engaged now, but there's no need to bring up any women from my past."

"Sorry Clarissa," Ethan said, looking sheepish.

She shrugged, not seeming concerned in the least as Blake's arm tightened around her.

Grayson looked over to Jackson. "But speaking of Raptor's neighbor, she did look a little freaked out. What were you helping her with?"

"The trash," he said with a low chuckle. "Her can was broken, and she said they wanted to charge her seventy dollars for a new one."

Grayson's eyes widened. "Seventy bucks? Damn. Raptor, what the hell kind of rich neighborhood is this?"

Blake glanced over at them in confusion but was focused on his Clarissa, more than content to murmur into her ear as she sat on his lap. Jackson looked back at his teammate. "It was weird. I get some women are intimidated by my size, and I'll admit I surprised her. I don't know. I just got the sense something was wrong."

Gray nodded. "You should ask Raptor about her. He'd probably know something."

"Yep. No doubt." Jackson crossed the living room and sank down into a plush chair, listening to the end of Ethan's story.

"Wait, no fair," Ethan's date pouted when he was done. "You tell us this crazy story and can't even tell us where you were?"

Ethan glanced over at her, smiling. "I told you, baby. That's how it always is with us."

"That makes it even crazier. And you're used to this?" she jokingly asked Clarissa.

Clarissa shook her head, her blonde hair catching the light. "I don't think I'll ever get used to it. We've only been together a few months though, so maybe I'm wrong. But I trust Blake and his team. They rescued me, you know."

"Rescued you? From what? I'm Donna, by the way."

The two women introduced themselves, and Jackson smirked. Of course Ethan's flavor of the week wouldn't know anything about Clarissa or the team. Not that he faulted the guy—they'd all chased after plenty of women over the years. Jackson had done the same damn thing. A new pretty girl each weekend was tempting as hell when you were young and single. When you were only concerned about getting laid, not getting into a serious relationship. He wasn't exactly old at thirty-one, but he sure as hell felt it sometimes compared to some of the other guys.

"I hope everyone's hungry," Blake said, changing the subject. "I've got steaks, burgers, and ribs to grill tonight."

"I insisted on the ribs," Clarissa said. "I've spent so much time here this summer, I was missing Texas BBQ."

"You need to get Blake here a smoker," Jackson said in amusement. "Otherwise, it just won't compare."

"I know. That's exactly what I told him," she lamented. "We don't have a ton of room outside though. This'll work for now."

Blake eyed the small deck. "I've been telling Clarissa we could get a bigger place now that she's officially moved in with me. Rent a house with a nice big backyard or something."

"This is fine," she said, standing up. Blake's hands were instantly at her waist, helping her.

"Sure," he said, rising as well. Jackson noticed he keep one hand lightly on her hip, as if he didn't want to let her go. "Fine for now," he continued. "But you'll work from home some of the time, right? So you'll want your own office. I wouldn't mind more space and a bigger yard."

"Are you going to keep teaching?" Jackson asked. Clarissa was a biologist and college professor who'd been conducting research when the team met her down in Colombia. "Met" wasn't exactly the right word, either. Blake had found her when they'd been running an op, chasing after a terrorist stashing chemical weapons. Clarissa had been kidnapped and held hostage in the damn camp. If Blake hadn't found her, Jackson hated to think what could've happened.

"I'll be teaching remotely for now. I still have my position in Texas, but they're willing to let me do the lectures online this semester. An assistant will be running the labs for me."

"Wow," Jackson said. "You must be really smart."

Blake chuckled. "Smarter than me, that's for damn sure. They didn't want to let her go."

"Lots of colleges have online classes now. The infrastructure is set up, so it's just a matter of moving my lecture to an online platform. I can adjust fairly easily. That reminds me. I was talking some more to our neighbor the other day. She's finishing up college and doing it one hundred percent virtually."

"Which neighbor?" Blake asked.

"Taryn. Right next door."

Grayson grinned. "Jackson was helping her out when Hailey and I pulled up. So, is she single or what?"

Blake briefly looked surprised but then glanced at him. "When'd you meet her? Tonight?"

Jackson nodded. "She seemed a little scared of me, to be honest. I pulled up in front of your house and saw her when I got out of my SUV. Maybe she assumed I was you," he said, lifting a shoulder.

Blake frowned. "She's quiet. I think Taryn's talked more to Clarissa than me."

"You're intimidating," Clarissa said.

Blake chuckled. "I can't be that damn intimidating. You just moved in with me and agreed to be my wife."

"I don't mean now. When you first burst into my tent, I was terrified."

Jackson watched as Blake stiffened. He knew his buddy still wanted to rip the hearts out of the men who'd kidnapped Clarissa. Hell, they all did. None of them would put up with a man harming a woman. Ever.

"Hey," Clarissa said quietly. "You saved me. I just

meant if a woman didn't know you, and was already skittish around men…." She trailed off. Jackson eyed her carefully, wondering if she'd had the same thoughts as him. Taryn had seemed skittish of him. That was exactly the right term. It was crazy though, because he didn't know the woman and didn't really know what she'd been thinking. He could've just caught her off guard.

The women continued to talk for a moment as Blake went out on the deck to light the grill. Logan walked over, and more introductions began with the women his teammates had brought. Jackson frowned, his gaze shifting to the window. Blake was outside, and he could see part of Taryn's deck right next door.

She'd seemed surprised when he'd invited her to join them, but it seemed silly for her to sit home alone. And he had assumed she was alone. No man would let his girlfriend or wife haul that huge broken trash can down to the curb.

His sense about things was usually correct, and he wondered again if Blake's neighbor might be hiding something. Being shy didn't mean you'd hesitate to say your own name.

"You look deep in thought," Clarissa commented.

"Just wondering about your neighbor."

"I should invite her over."

"I did," Jackson said with a low chuckle. "Ghost and Hailey pulled up when I was talking to her, so it just seemed like the right thing to do."

"And?"

"She declined."

"I should quick go over and talk to her. I don't think she knows many people here. Besides, I'd love to get to know her more since she's right next door. I didn't have many close friends in Texas, just work colleagues. Now that I'm teaching virtually, I don't even have that connection."

"She'd probably like that," Jackson agreed. "I don't know her, obviously, but just got the sense that she was alone."

Troy and his date finally came in from the kitchen, both of them grinning ear to ear as they joined the rest of the group. Jackson smirked as his gaze ran over the woman's mussed up hair. That must have been one hell of a kiss.

"Nice of you to join us," Ethan quipped. "We thought we'd need to get you two a room."

"She's got me wrapped around her finger," Troy said as the blonde woman giggled. "I can't keep my hands to myself."

"Don't worry, we noticed," Blake said dryly, walking back in. He immediately went to Clarissa's side, and Jackson watched as she leaned against him. They were so natural together; it was a little hard to believe they'd only been dating a few months and were now engaged. Blake had always been more than happy to go out to bars with the team and take a woman home for the night. But now? He only had eyes for Clarissa, the two of them looked happier than hell.

Jackson was glad his SEAL team leader had found the right woman for him. It didn't make his own lack of a love life any easier though. He took a swig of his beer, his eyes taking in the room full of his friends.

"Who said I was worried?" Troy laughed, wrapping his arm around his date's waist. "But we're in here now and ready to celebrate you two shacking up."

Blake guffawed as Clarissa blushed, but he took her hand and kissed the back of it, ignoring the ribbing of his teammates.

"Oh, let me get a look at your ring!" Hailey said, rushing over to her. "The last time I saw you was when everyone helped move my stuff into Grayson's apartment. You hadn't even been ring shopping yet."

"Yeah, let me get a look, too," Grayson quipped.

Hailey rolled her eyes, playfully swatting at him. "You don't care about her ring," she teased.

"Nope, but I do want to see what you like."

Hailey turned red as everyone around them chuckled. Ghost and Hailey's relationship had been quick as well. She'd been working in Bagram when he'd come to her rescue, and they'd reconnected when she moved out to San Diego for her next assignment. They weren't engaged yet, but Hailey had just moved in with him. Jackson had a feeling both of his teammates would be hitched within the next year or so.

"Welcome to the team, Clarissa," Troy said with a wink as everyone gathered around, the women oohing and aahing over the diamond.

"It's good to be here," she said, flushing slightly as all eyes were on them. "I know I was here over the summer, but now I've officially moved."

"And I'm glad you're mine," Raptor said possessively.

"Hoorah!" Ethan whooped.

"And as much as I like all of you," Clarissa said, looking around at the men, "I hope we never ride in a helicopter together ever again."

Troy chuckled, and Jackson recalled how Troy had been the one to bring her up from the jungles of

Colombia, Clarissa strapped in to the harness beside him as they dangled from a rope. "Aw," Troy said. "You were amazing."

Blake growled, and Troy held up his hands in mock surrender. "Easy Raptor," he joked. "Your woman did great on our little adventure."

"Little adventure?" Hailey asked with a laugh. "If it was anything like when I met Grayson, I understand why she'd want to forget."

"Exactly," Clarissa joked.

"But then we wouldn't have met you two," Grayson said.

"Damn straight," Blake agreed, tugging his fiancée even closer to his side.

"Yeah, yeah, enough chit chat," Troy joked. "Now on to the important stuff. When's dinner?"

Chapter 2

Taryn Miller shakily shut the front door to her townhouse, wondering how the hell she hadn't noticed the massive man next door. She'd realized someone was there, sure, but she'd naively assumed it was her neighbor Blake. And she knew better than to assume anything, especially when it came to her safety and letting her guard down. That's how people got hurt. How she'd put herself in danger.

She locked the deadbolt and put on the chain, finally turning and walking into her kitchen.

Her neighbor Blake seemed like a decent enough guy. He'd been preoccupied over this summer with his girlfriend and otherwise had mostly kept to himself. He went on his missions for the Navy, didn't pry in her life, and was generally just polite yet reserved when he saw her.

She didn't know him well but was familiar enough with him to know he'd never harm her.

If Austin ever did find her, she hoped Blake was the type of man who would come running if he heard her screaming for help next door. He had a girlfriend now though. Fiancée, actually. And he deployed an awful lot. She didn't need to drag them into her business, even if he was the sort to step in if someone needed him.

And that new guy tonight? Jackson?

She shuddered slightly, both in fear and attraction.

He was huge, with large biceps that had stretched the sleeves of his shirt and broad shoulders. He was even taller than Blake, impossible as it seemed. And with his dark hair and intense gaze, he was intimidating as hell. He was more than a foot taller than her, exactly the type of man she was afraid of. A guy like him wouldn't need a weapon or anything to hurt her—his sheer strength alone would be enough to do serious damage to her petite frame.

He'd walked over to help her tonight without even waiting for a response. He probably had a girlfriend or something with the way he'd so casually offered to assist, like it was no big deal.

Maybe it wasn't.

Her trash can was broken, much like the other things she needed to repair in her house. The lightbulb in the foyer was out—which wouldn't be a big deal if she had a ladder. The sink in the kitchen drained more slowly than she liked. She'd tried to snake it once but hadn't been too successful, and she didn't want to go back to the hardware store to buy something else. A plumber would certainly cost an arm and a leg.

She should borrow a ladder from someone though, maybe even one of her neighbors. The more lights she had working in her house, the better. She shouldn't take any risks when it came to her safety.

Blowing out a sigh, she looked around her small kitchen. A sliding glass door led to the deck, and she could hear the sound of laughter from right next door.

The party Jackson had been going to.

She'd never had a group of people over here—never could, really. Not while Austin was still looking for her. The more people she befriended, the more likely she'd be in danger. Austin had cop friends all over the place. She knew he'd never rest until he found her.

She said hello to her neighbors but hadn't really talked much to any of them, except for Clarissa. It was silly of her to trust a woman she didn't know, but Clarissa had been kidnapped over the summer. If anyone understood her fears or some of what she'd been through, it would be her. Not that she'd confided in the woman. But she had spoken more to her than anyone else in the past year.

It was silly to even think about the men and their dates next door. She couldn't befriend them. The more she kept to herself, the safer she'd be. If she went to a party, people could take pictures, post them online—anything.

She had an anonymous social media account—a different fake name with no photo. It was mostly so she could keep tabs on her ex.

But as for Jackson?

She hadn't missed the spark of interest in his eyes. A guy like that could protect her, no doubt. He was huge and would intimate most people with a single look. If he was in the Navy, possibly even a SEAL, like she suspected of her neighbor, he could easily do Austin harm. Shield her from his blows if he ever did find her.

Too bad she was too damn afraid of Jackson and his friends to even ask for their help.

Opening her fridge, she stared at the sparse contents—milk, lettuce, and a package of bologna. She wouldn't get paid for her freelance design work until next week, so until then, she'd have to survive on the few items in her fridge and pantry. She was a whiz at graphic design, and it enabled her to work from home, but not many people were willing to pay her under the table.

She couldn't use her real name or social security number. She didn't pay taxes. All of those things would make it too easy for Austin to find her.

Closing her eyes, she wished once more that she had a normal life. That she could work in a real office and meet people. That she could take on more client work at home without anyone getting suspicious. She loved what she did, but taking a few jobs now and then wasn't a career. And she knew she couldn't live in this neighborhood forever anyway. It was safer for her if she kept moving. Running. It was no way to live, but what choice did she have?

Taryn heard the roar of laughter again, and hastened a glance outside. She couldn't really see that well from here. Blake had a privacy screen built in to his deck. It had already been there when he moved in, but she could see people moving around through the hatching.

Their decks were so close together, being in a townhouse community, someone could probably leap from one deck to another if they wanted. Not that she'd ever try it, but it creeped her out knowing someone could come in the back door like that.

She didn't need to worry at this exact moment though—no one would try sneaking in to her townhouse from the deck when there was a huge group next door.

She cracked the sliding glass door, letting in some fresh air, and walked back into her kitchen. And who was she kidding—the sounds of voices and laughter coming from her neighbor's house made her feel less alone. Her stomach rumbled as the scent of charcoal wafted through the air, and suddenly tears smarted her eyes.

When was the last time she'd had a grilled burger or steak?

She'd never have a normal life again—normal friends, a normal job. She couldn't let herself get close to anyone when she might be putting them in danger. She had no doubt that whenever Austin found her, he'd hurt whoever she was with. He wouldn't have any qualms about hurting another person just to get to her. Shoot. He'd probably enjoy it.

For a cop, he had a very dark side.

She jumped as her doorbell rang, startling her from her thoughts, and she frantically looked around.

Sheesh.

Did normal people get freaked out like that just from a doorbell? Just because she'd been thinking of her ex-husband didn't mean he was here. And really—it's not like he'd politely ring the doorbell.

Taryn wasn't expecting anyone, so she decided to just ignore it. Hopefully whoever was there would just go away. The bell rang again though, and she thought she heard women's voices outside. Padding across the kitchen, she peeked out between the blinds.

Clarissa. Blake's new girlfriend. There was a second woman she didn't recognize beside her.

They probably knew she was home since she'd just been outside.

Pulling the sliding glass door and ensuring it was locked, she made her way to the front door to see what they wanted. Maybe they needed some ice or something for their party. That was about all she could offer anyway with her empty kitchen.

She undid the chain, wondering if they'd question why she'd taken so long to answer. Pulling the door open a crack, Taryn watched as Clarissa smiled at her. "Hi! We just wanted to come invite you over for dinner. Blake is grilling tons of food—more even than those guys can eat," she added with a laugh. "And I know you don't know us very well, but a few of the guys brought dates over, too."

"I'm Donna," the other woman said with a friendly smile. "I don't know anyone aside from Ethan."

"I don't know," Taryn said uncertainly. "But I wouldn't want to intrude."

"It's no intrusion," Clarissa assured her. "The guys all know each other from base, but I've barely met the other women. Besides, I just moved here and would love to make some new friends."

Taryn nodded, uneasiness creeping through her. She did like Clarissa. They'd chatted a few times and talked about school. Taryn was taking some online classes but not actually finishing her degree. How could she, when she couldn't use her real name?

Clarissa taught at a college though, and she seemed interested in learning how Taryn liked online classes since that was what she'd be teaching via the Internet this semester.

"Did you get your schedule settled for fall?" Clarissa asked.

"Oh, uh, yeah. I'm just taking two classes virtually."

"I have to admit teaching online courses is a bit of a learning curve for me. With some of my bigger lectures, I can't even see all the students' faces. Sometimes I feel like I'm just sitting there talking to myself."

Taryn smiled. "It's different than actual class. I've got a laptop and separate monitor so I can watch on one screen and work on the other. I kind of need to with graphic design though."

"That makes perfect sense. I'm still figuring out my set up. But seriously, come on over," Clarissa said again. "We've got tons of food. Just come say hi—I promise the guys are all really nice."

"You'd be doing me a favor," Donna said with a wink. "I don't know anyone but Ethan really."

"Oh. Um, sure, I guess," she said as Clarissa and Donna just stood there. "Maybe just for a little while. I'll come over in a few minutes."

"Awesome. I'll let Blake and the guys know you're coming. We'll see you soon!" Clarissa waved, and then she walked back down the steps with Donna, crossing the yard to Blake's house. Well, Blake and Clarissa's house now. For a moment, Taryn wondered why they were having a BBQ on a Sunday evening. Maybe the guys had just gotten back from another mission or something.

Closing the door, she went to slip on her sandals and grab her keys. As much as she didn't want to go, meeting her neighbors was probably a good idea, even if she didn't make a habit of hanging out with them. Blake might travel a lot, but she'd like to have a female friend. She could never truly confide in her, of course, but they could talk about classes and such.

And as for the tall and mysterious guy who'd helped her?

She had to admit that Jackson intrigued her. He was big and strong, but the intense way he looked at her had sent her heart fluttering.

She'd never date him of course. Not that he'd want to date her. But she couldn't help but feel like she'd be safe with him. A guy like that could protect her from her ex-husband, not that she'd ever drag him into something like that.

And she could sense immediately that he was nothing like Austin. He was confident, sure, but not in an obnoxious way. He'd helped her but hadn't stood there leering at her. He hadn't done anything to make her uncomfortable, just hauled her trash down and then gone into his friend's house. And besides, she was going next door to see Clarissa. Jackson would be there, sure, but so would an entire group of people.

She could ignore the tiny spark of interest she'd felt when he'd looked at her.

She hadn't dated anyone, ever, aside from her ex. Some men could probably be trusted, but she sure wouldn't ever find out.

Glancing around her townhouse, she decided to leave on a few more lights. She probably wouldn't stay long, but just in case, she didn't want to come home to a dark townhouse. It was hard enough sleeping at night as it was, with every sound keeping her awake.

Maybe someday she'd feel safe again—years from now.

Not enough time had passed yet since she'd run, and she knew Austin was looking for her.

Ten minutes later, she was finally crossing over toward Blake and Clarissa's. It had only taken a moment to get ready, but she didn't want to appear too eager. How silly was that? It's not like she was doing anything home alone. She heard laughter coming from out back and wondered if they'd even hear her knocking on the door. It's not like they were sitting around with bated breath, waiting for her to show up.

Taryn climbed the steps to the front door, identical to her own townhouse. She was shocked when it swung open before she'd even knocked. Jackson stepped back, seeming like he didn't want to frighten her, but her heart pounded in her chest. She'd assumed Clarissa or Blake would open the door, not the man who'd come over to help her earlier.

"Everyone's out back," he said, his voice deep. "I told Raptor I'd let you in."

"I didn't bring anything," she said nervously.

"There's no need. You only had a few minutes notice, and trust me, they've got enough food to feed the entire street."

"Okay," she said uncertainly, still standing in place.

His dark eyes met hers, but he didn't move. Didn't pressure her to come inside. She had a feeling that if she'd turned around and left, walking back to her own townhouse, he wouldn't follow her or be upset. He'd just recognize that she wasn't ready to come over after all.

As it was, he simply stood there towering above her, not getting too close, but sending her senses in high alert nonetheless.

"You're safe here," he said in a low voice. She blanched, quickly covering the surprise she was sure was written all over her face. What made him think she felt unsafe? It couldn't be that obvious. Clarissa certainly hadn't seemed to notice her unease much of the time.

"Oh, um…."

"Why don't you come in. Can I get you a drink?" he continued, acting like it was perfectly normal to tell someone they were safe when they first arrived at your home.

"Water is fine."

He nodded and stepped back as she finally came inside, closing the door behind her. She jumped as he turned the deadbolt, her gaze moving from it to him. "Everyone's here already, so I locked up."

She nodded, still feeling wary.

"Would you feel more comfortable if I left it unlocked? With six Navy SEALs here, I'm sure Raptor won't care. It's just a habit."

"No, it's fine," she said, feeling silly. "I'm just…nervous I guess."

"There's no need to be."

Jackson gestured for her to go ahead of him, so she turned and walked into the living room. He was huge, towering above her, but he didn't follow too closely, seeming to recognize that she needed her space. Most of the others were out back on the small deck, but she saw one couple quietly talking on the sofa.

"We've got soda, bottles of water, beer, too. There are also a couple bottles of wine if you're a wine drinker. Some of the women prefer that."

"Maybe later. I don't want to drink on an empty stomach."

He frowned, moving past her to the fridge, and pulled out a bottle of water for her. "You made it!" Clarissa called out from the deck, waving as she spotted them. She was holding a huge platter of food for Blake as he put some of it on the grill. The others were talking and laughing, enjoying themselves. She spotted a few large guys tipping back their bottles of beer, but Clarissa had been right. There were several other women here as well.

She waved back at Clarissa and twisted the cap off her water bottle, taking a sip. "What's wrong?" she asked, noticing Jackson still watching her.

"Nothing. I was just worried that you hadn't eaten anything."

She raised her eyebrows.

"Ignore me," he said with a low chuckle. "Why don't I introduce you to everyone? Clarissa's busy helping Blake with the food at the moment, but I'll introduce you to the other guys. I'm sure she'll be done in a minute."

"Okay," she said softly, looking out at the deck filled with people. Her hands trembled slightly as she took another sip of water, and she wondered if Jackson would notice. She was nervous, yes, but she also hadn't eaten much today.

"Taryn."

Her gaze flicked back toward him.

His voice was low and calming. She liked how he said her name, the way it sent butterflies fluttering in her stomach and heat coursing through her. She could never get close to a man like him, obviously, but for a brief second, she pretended she was normal. That she could date and have a normal life, a normal boyfriend. That she wasn't on the run, hiding from a man who'd stop at nothing to hurt her.

All men weren't like Austin. Rationally, she realized that, even if she was cautious all of the time. These guys were big and strong, but if anything, they'd help her. If she was in trouble, she should be happy to be in a room full of military men, not scared.

Jackson cleared his throat. "I know I'm a big guy, and I can intimidate people," he said, his voice low and deep. "You seem a little nervous, which is understandable since you don't know us, well, you don't know me at all. But I swear I'd never hurt you," he said seriously. "None of the guys here would. You already know that we're military. We train together and fight for our country. Sure, we can be a little loud and rough around the edges, but you don't ever need to be scared around me or any of my friends. I get the feeling you're a little wary, and although I'd like to know why, I won't push. Just know that I'd never lay a hand on you."

She nodded, blinking away the sudden wetness in her eyes.

How had he guessed she was terrified of him?

His gaze softened slightly as he watched her, but he didn't comment on her nearly being in tears. He didn't say anything else, just seemed content for his words to sink in. She pulled herself together, straightening her back.

"Thank you."

"You can talk to me if you ever need a friend. I

mean, hell. I admit that I'm attracted to you, but I'd never pressure a woman into anything. And Clarissa invited you over because she genuinely wanted to get to know you. So did I, if I'm being completely honest. I didn't like the fear in your eyes that I saw earlier. Hopefully you'll tell me about that sometime, but just know, Blake and Clarissa would bend over backwards to help you if you're in some sort of trouble."

"I just—I don't trust people I don't know."

"Fair enough," he said easily.

"I do like Clarissa though. I mean—not that I dislike the rest of you." His lips quirked, and she bumbled forward. "I just don't really know Blake. He was always coming and going and a bit intimidating. Clarissa is easy to talk to and seems really genuine."

"She is," he said, taking a pull of his beer. "She gets along with everyone, and if anything, can be a little too trusting. I don't know if she's told you her story yet."

Taryn shook her head no.

"Well, maybe I'll leave the details to her. But let's just say, we met her while my team was on an op over the summer. Blake rescued her, and she knows us better than most people after being in that situation."

"Wow. I honestly had no idea."

"She's special to Blake, and likewise, to the rest of us because of it. We'd protect her if harm came her way again. Not that she's in danger," he hurriedly assured Taryn. "Just know that we watch out for people we care about."

"You don't know me."

"No, but I'd like to get to know you. I can appreciate that you're cautious though and don't want to share a lot about yourself. How about I go introduce you to the others?"

"You're not going to ask me any questions?" she said, confused.

Jackson pressed his lips together. "Not if it makes you uncomfortable."

A beat passed, and she saw nothing but sincerity in his dark eyes. It would be hard trusting anyone with her secrets. She knew that she never could. But this was just a party. A BBQ with her neighbors. She could attempt to relax for an hour or so and get to know them better. She didn't have to ever see the rest of them again.

She nodded as he watched her. "Okay. I'd like to meet everyone."

Chapter 3

Jackson chuckled an hour later, listening to the guys rib one another. Troy and his date had split early, but the rest of them were hanging around chatting. The women were all sitting together at the outdoor table while the guys stood nearby, and the rest of the food was almost ready.

"So where do you work?" he heard Taryn ask Hailey.

"I work for the DOD—Department of Defense."

"You work with them?" Taryn asked, looking toward the men, confused.

"Oh no, these guys are military. I'm a civilian employee, and I'm in a separate building than where they are on base. I did meet Grayson when we were both working in Afghanistan though."

"You weren't kidnapped, too, were you?"

"No, but I was working in Bagram on a year-long DOD assignment. These guys were there for a short-term thing, and there was a suicide bombing and explosion—"

"Oh my God, I heard about that! That huge bombing. Sorry, I didn't mean to interrupt," Taryn quickly added.

"You're fine," Hailey assured her. "I met Grayson right in the middle of the chaos."

"Wow, I can't even imagine," Taryn said. "That must have been terrifying."

"It was," Hailey agreed. "The explosion actually knocked me out, so I mostly remember Grayson carrying me to safety. It's kind of crazy that Clarissa and I each met one of the guys on the team when they were working." Her gaze flicked over to Jackson. "It looks like you seem to have already caught the attention of one of them."

Taryn flushed, and Jackson liked the hint of pink spreading across her cheeks. "Don't tease her," he said easily.

The women looked over and laughed, Taryn the only one looking surprised that he'd been listening in. "I told you," Hailey said, winking at Jackson.

He smirked and looked back at his buddies. "She seems to be getting along with the other women," Logan commented.

"Yep. Apparently, Clarissa befriended her this summer. I don't think they've ever hung out before tonight though."

"She's quiet," Ethan commented. "Then again, so are you. It'd be a match made in heaven."

"She's reserved," Jackson said in a low voice. "She seems a bit wary—maybe just because she doesn't know us. I'm a little surprised Clarissa even got her to come over. I asked her earlier, and she shot me down."

"Maybe she got burned in the past," Logan said, taking a pull of his beer. "She looks young, but hell. Plenty of men are assholes."

Jackson frowned. His friends had all noticed the same thing he did—she was a bit wary around them. It could've just been because she didn't know them. Hell, she barely knew Blake, and he was her neighbor. And plenty of guys were after only one thing—getting into a woman's pants. She didn't really have a reason to trust him yet.

He didn't like that she'd seemed uncertain about all six of them though. He was attracted to Taryn, sure, but it didn't escape his notice that she seemed infinitely more comfortable around all the women.

"Any word from the CO?" Ethan asked, changing the subject.

Blake shook his head. "Negative. Ace's team just went to Nigeria to rescue an American citizen there. The guys in Little Creek are on an op, too. Anything new that comes up is probably us. And there are still the two missing women in Afghanistan."

Jackson nodded. There were always multiple situations unfolding around the world that required their attention. He never knew if he'd have hours or days before a mission. He even kept a go bag in his car with a change of clothes and a few small necessities in case he needed to be back on base ASAP.

He'd gotten used to the life of a SEAL. He didn't have anyone waiting for him at home, so up and leaving at a moment's notice hadn't ever been a problem. Briefly, he wondered how Raptor and Ghost would handle it with their women. Clarissa had been with Blake over the summer, even if not officially moved in, so she must have some clue about their deployments. Ghost and Hailey were in a new relationship though. What would she think when they had to deploy?

It was hard on members of the Special Forces—and part of the damn reason he was still single. Women didn't like his disappearing act, even if he didn't have a choice in the matter. Maybe he'd be gone a few days, but sometimes it was a couple of weeks or longer. He couldn't tell them where he was going. When he returned, he couldn't say where he'd been. And he knew it had to be hell on those they left behind.

"Time to check on the food," Blake said, grabbing a pair of tongs and crossing toward the grill He lifted the lid, the amazing smell of grilled food filling the air.

He lived in a small apartment himself and wouldn't mind someday renting a townhouse where he had a deck and yard.

"So how come you didn't bring a date tonight?" Jackson asked, his gaze shifting to Logan.

He chuckled. "I was going to, but damn. All the women I've been with lately are just too much drama."

"How much drama can one night with them be?" Jackson asked with a smirk.

"Damn," Logan said with a laugh. "One night has always suited me just fine. I'm having fun at least. But introducing a woman to all of you would give her ideas that I want more than just a night."

"Gotcha," Jackson said.

"I can't believe Troy bugged out early though."

Jackson raised his eyebrows. "What's not to

believe? He was all over that chick he was with."

"Noted. Why wait for dinner when he could take her home and feast on pussy instead?"

Jackson nearly choked on his beer. He knew Logan was joking, mostly. But Troy and his date couldn't keep their hands off of each other. He had a feeling neither of them minded leaving early to get on with the later part of their evening.

Jesus.

Nowadays, Jackson preferred getting to know a woman before taking her to bed. He was getting too old for the bar scene and sleeping with a stranger he'd just met. Not that he saw himself settling down anytime soon. Maybe he was simply better off being alone.

"The steaks and ribs are ready!" Blake said loudly, carrying over a huge platter of food to a side table he'd set up. Chips and side dishes were spread across it as well, and Jackson's stomach rumbled. He'd gotten in a five-mile run this afternoon, even though it was a Sunday, and he was starving.

"I hope everyone's hungry after eating all those burgers," Clarissa said, eyeing the empty plate where the burgers had been.

"Have you met us?" Ethan quipped. "Of course we're still hungry."

"I don't like that you didn't eat yet," Blake murmured in a low voice, moving to Clarissa's side. Hell. Jackson could appreciate that. Blake was protective of his woman. She'd been through a lot over the summer, and the stress from moving and such had been weighing on her as well.

Clarissa smiled at him though. "You know I've been waiting for the ribs."

"A Texas girl at heart," Blake joked. He glanced at the other women. "Ladies first. I'll hold off the guys until you help yourselves."

The women walked over, and Jackson noticed Taryn hanging back to let the others go ahead of her. He grabbed a plate and stood behind her, noticing she smelled faintly of roses as her hair blew in the breeze. His cock instantly hardened.

Fuck she was gorgeous.

That white tee-shirt set off her dark hair and ivory skin. She was petite but had curves in exactly the right places. She was at least a foot shorter than him, and something about that made his protective instincts soar. He had half a mind to pull her into his chest and shield her from the world.

Where that thought had come from, he didn't even want to know.

He made sure not to stand too close behind her and watched as she took a steak and some potato salad.

"That's my favorite, too," he commented.

"I can't remember the last time I had steak," she said wistfully. "It smells amazing."

Jackson frowned, wondering why she never had it. "You don't like to grill?" he asked, helping himself to some food.

"I don't have one."

He nodded. It wasn't too surprising, he supposed. Some women just weren't into that sort of thing. Plus, he'd found out earlier that she was indeed single. There was no boyfriend that was deployed. No husband stationed somewhere. It was just her.

Why that intrigued him so much, he didn't want to examine too closely.

He wasn't looking for a relationship.

"So, Clarissa said you're a graphic designer," he commented, filling his own plate.

"Oh, um, yes. I design all sorts of things— websites, logos, branding for companies. I don't have a degree but have done it for years."

"I can't even use Photoshop," Jackson said with a chuckle.

"Nah, but you could kill a man with your bare hands," Ethan quipped.

Taryn paled, and the two men exchanged a glance. "Hell, I'm sorry," Ethan said. "I was just joking around. Jackson would never hurt someone who didn't deserve it. None of us would."

"Are you okay?" Clarissa asked, looking concerned as she glanced over.

"Fine. Yeah," Taryn murmured.

"Taryn," Jackson said in a low voice. He reached out and took her plate of food, noticing the way her hands trembled again. She looked flustered and somewhat embarrassed by her reaction. "Go ahead and sit down," he said quietly. "I'll bring this over."

She nodded, biting her lip, but rather than taking a seat at the table again, went inside to the living room. The other women were gathering around the table outside, laughing and talking, although Clarissa still looked concerned. Jackson exchanged a glance with Blake. "I'll make sure she's okay," Jackson assured him.

He carried his own plate inside along with Taryn's, setting them both down on the coffee table. "Are you all right?" he asked, sinking down into a chair across from the sofa. She looked surprised for a beat, but it was the least threatening place he could think of to be. He didn't want to sit beside her. If he stood, he'd tower above her. And he didn't feel right about leaving her inside alone.

She eyed the plate of food, her stomach rumbling.

"Go ahead," he said. "I came in to make sure you're okay."

"Sorry about that," she said, looking embarrassed again. She reached out and took her plate, setting it on her lap. He'd grabbed utensils for them as well, and he watched as she daintily sliced off a piece of her steak. She brushed a lock of her dark hair behind one ear, and he found himself fascinated by how fragile she looked. Taryn had delicate features—high cheekbones and those deep brown eyes, set off even more by her fair skin, small hands, and even dainty little feet peeking out of her sandals.

He felt huge next to her, like a hulking giant or something. At six-foot-five, he easily stood above other men. He towered over Taryn though. She was at least a foot shorter than him. Something about that appealed to his base instincts. He liked knowing he could shield her from danger and protect her. Provide for her. His cock stirred at the idea of making love to her. She was so small, he'd have to always be careful, but the idea of bending her over and taking her from behind while he claimed her was appealing as hell.

What would it sound like if she whimpered his name, crying out as he brought her to the peaks of pleasure?

He needed to get his mind out of the gutter though. Ethan's comment had upset her, and it's not like he was about to take her to bed.

Jackson dug into his own food, frowning as he heard her stomach rumble.

"Sorry," she said, flushing again. "I didn't eat much today."

"Why not?" he asked, not caring that he was being somewhat rude. She was slender with nice curves, but he hoped she wasn't on some sort of crash diet or something. Taryn was gorgeous. She didn't need to diet.

"Oh, I just need to get to the store," she said, looking flustered.

He nodded, not convinced that was really the reason. It was Sunday evening after all. Most people did their grocery shopping on the weekends. Although, if she worked from home, maybe she went out and ran errands during the week. He was sure there were some benefits to a flexible schedule like that where she did design working from home. He was at the mercy of the Navy, on base early, and putting in long hours when duty called.

Hell.

It would be nice having a woman like Taryn there when he got home.

Resisting the urge to groan, he took a bite of his food. He didn't need the complications a woman and relationship would bring into his life.

"Hi guys!" Clarissa said, walking in. "Can I get you a beer or something, Taryn? A glass of wine? We have sodas, too, if you'd prefer."

"Do you have any red?" Taryn asked hesitantly.

"We sure do," Clarissa assured her. "I'll be right back."

"Damn, Blake knows how to grill a good steak," Jackson said, taking another bite. He glanced over and was pleased to see that Taryn actually was eating.

"Yeah, this is amazing."

"You could put a grill out on your deck," Jackson said, nodding toward the balcony doors.

"Well, I don't know how to use a charcoal grill. I know they have those small portable ones, but…." She shrugged. "I'd probably just make a mess of things and ruin the food. And I'm sure gas grills are really expensive."

He nodded, watching Clarissa walk back into the room. He'd been about ready to offer to teach her how to grill over charcoal, which was weird. If he really did teach her, then they'd probably eat together. Again.

"Here you go," Clarissa said, handing Taryn a glass of red. She held one as well and took a sip. "Wow, this is delicious. Hailey, this is amazing! Thanks!" she called out. Hailey waved from the deck, and Jackson assumed she and Ghost had brought the bottle.

Clarissa turned back to Taryn. "Maybe we can have a girls' night sometime now that I've officially moved in! I hardly know anyone out here. Hailey is from the DC area and just moved to San Diego as well. Honestly, I didn't have a ton of close girlfriends back in Texas. It would be nice having a friend right next door."

Taryn nodded, appearing to relax slightly. "Yeah, that would be fun."

"Maybe when the guys are gone, I'll have everyone over," Clarissa said. "Otherwise, Blake will just be hovering."

"He seems protective of you," Taryn noticed.

"Yeah, he definitely is. I'm used to being independent, but I honestly don't mind. Oh, geez, let me see what they need. Excuse me," she said, hurrying back out the door to see what Blake was gesturing about. Jackson had nearly finished his food, and he was happy to see Taryn had eaten as well.

"You doing okay?" Jackson asked quietly.

"Yeah. This is nice," she said, looking around. "I don't know a lot of people out here in San Diego, so I never go to parties or anything. I had to move here quickly—" She abruptly stopped talking, her face turning pale.

"Hey, it's all right," he assured her, resting his forearms on his legs and leaning closer. He wanted to reach out and touch her, comfort her, but he didn't think that would be welcomed. "You don't have to tell me. That doesn't mean I don't want to know, just that I understand if you'd prefer not to say."

"I don't talk about myself much," she said softly.

Jackson nodded. "I don't either."

She relaxed slightly and took a sip of the wine. "Clarissa was right—this is really good."

"I'll find out what kind it is," he said.

They talked a few more minutes as the others finished eating and began carrying their plates inside. The sun was beginning to sink in the sky, and Jackson could sense Taryn was growing nervous again. "I should head out before it gets too late," she said, her gaze looking out the balcony doors.

Jackson's lips quirked. "You're right next door."

"Yeah, I know. I just like to be careful."

He nodded. Was she just looking for an excuse to leave? Or was walking next door in the dark an actual concern for her? "Would it be all right if I walked you home?" he found himself asking.

She looked surprised for a moment but nodded, looking slightly relieved. "Okay. I'd prefer it actually. I don't like walking alone at night."

Jackson stilled, wondering exactly what she meant by that. He knew most women wouldn't feel comfortable walking around alone in the dark, but she was literally right next door. This was a well-lit, safe neighborhood. Why was she frightened just to go to her own house? Not for the first time, Jackson wondered what she was hiding.

Taryn said goodbye to everyone, and Jackson told his friends he'd be right back. A moment later, he was opening Raptor's front door and following Taryn down the steps. He tried not to stare at her ass in those jeans, but damn. She was gorgeous.

The wind lightly blew her hair, and he caught the briefest hint of a rose scent again. His groin tightened, but he ignored it. He was just seeing her safely home, not pulling her into his arms and kissing her like he wanted. Jackson was attracted to her, but his need to see to her safety overrode any other thought. For some reason, she was frightened, and he didn't like the uneasiness that stirred inside of him.

They crossed over to her yard, not saying a word, and then a police car slowly drove down the street. Taryn stiffened beside him, and Jackson frowned. Was she in some sort of trouble with the law? He didn't get that vibe from her at all, but she'd noticeably reacted. The police car continued on its way, and Taryn hurried toward her townhouse.

Jackson followed her up the steps to her front door. He didn't go all the way to the porch, instead stopping on the top step. Taryn turned and looked up at him. They were closer in height with him standing on the steps, but he was still taller than her.

"Is everything okay?" he asked.

She took a deep breath, nodding, but tears smarted

her eyes.

"You want to tell me what that was about?" Jackson asked, cocking his head in the direction the police car had driven. "You froze when you saw the police car. Are you in some sort of trouble?"

"My ex was a cop," she whispered. She swiped a tear off her cheek.

Jackson narrowed his eyes as he realized she was trembling. She was actually afraid of her ex. Scared enough that she was shaking. Something swelled within his chest that he couldn't quite explain—the need to hold her close and keep her safe. Erase that look of fear in her eyes.

He didn't have the right to touch her though. As much as he wanted to pull her into his embrace right now, he knew she'd never let him. He'd scare her more if he did something like that, which was concerning.

"Does he live here in San Diego?" Jackson asked.

"No." Her voice was barely a whisper. He searched her gaze. Her ex didn't even live nearby, and she was still terrified. Her lips parted slightly, and he had the strangest urge to cup her face and run his thumb over her mouth, soothing her.

"Did he hurt you?" Jackson asked, stiffening.

"It doesn't matter," she said, shaking her head. "Thank you for walking me back. I should go." She quickly turned, fumbling with the keys to her front door. Jackson wanted to reach out and stop her, to grab hold of her arm, but he felt paralyzed. He'd frighten her more if he tried to touch her.

The door swung open, and then she was stepping inside, Jackson still there on her front steps.

He hadn't moved a muscle, and it took everything

in him to stand there. To not go after her asking for more information. He was a man of action. He rushed into battle without thought to his own safety. His job was the mission, and he didn't sit on the sidelines waiting for someone else to take charge. He'd battled with terrorists and took lives without remorse in the name of duty to his country. But this one small woman had him afraid to so much as move a muscle. Just reaching out to comfort her might spook her more.

She turned to close the door, and he hated the look of sheer terror on her face. She was breathing rapidly, her hands shaking, and he couldn't do a damn thing.

"Let me help you," he said.

She shook her head, a stray tear running down her cheek. "Goodnight."

"Make sure you lock up," he said quietly as she began to shut the door.

"I will."

He heard the key in the lock turning and the sound of the chain, and he briefly wondered if Taryn was standing there looking at him through the peephole. He nodded at the door, just in case, but then he turned and jogged down the steps, his gut churning as he wondered what the hell he could do to help her.

Chapter 4

Taryn padded downstairs to her kitchen the next morning, laptop in hand. She needed to check her work emails and finalize the website she was working on. If the client approved her redesign, she could send them the final invoice. Hopefully they'd pay her right away, and then she could stock up at the grocery store. She did have an emergency credit card she could use to buy food, but what if Austin managed to track her with it?

She'd rather go hungry and make do with what she had in her kitchen than risk him finding her.

Last night she'd been almost paralyzed with fear when the police car had driven by. It was ridiculous for her to assume it was her ex-husband or even someone who knew him—not all cops were crooked. She knew that, logically.

That didn't stop her heart from pounding every time she was near a police officer though. Just seeing a man in a police uniform reminded her of Austin—how he'd come home from work already angry at her. He'd shove her out of his way. Hit her if she said the wrong thing. She was always relieved when he went to work for the day and terrified the moment he came home.

And Jackson.

God.

He'd seen how scared she was yesterday. It was embarrassing as hell to know he'd seen her frightened like that. He was a big, tough Navy SEAL. He'd said they'd rescued Clarissa. She didn't even want to imagine what nightmare scenario that was. Although she didn't know much about the military, she'd seen movies and TV shows. The SEALs went where other people couldn't.

What would he think of her being terrified of a single man?

And goodness. She'd have had a full-blown panic attack if Jackson hadn't been with her. She'd been scared enough despite having the muscular man right at her side. He was big and strong and made her stomach flip every time she looked at him.

Taryn hadn't been attracted to a man in a long time. She couldn't imagine ever dating again, but that didn't stop her skin from heating when he was near her.

She made herself a weak cup of coffee to conserve the little she had left and then got some peanut butter and crackers out of the cupboard. It wasn't typical breakfast food, but it had protein and calories. And despite eating the steak last night for dinner, her stomach rumbled.

Grimacing as she took a sip of the coffee, she

decided she'd make a stronger pot tomorrow. If she ran out of coffee, she ran out. This tasted awful.

She reviewed all the files for her website redesign one last time. She'd tweaked a few things over the weekend, and it looked perfect now. She uploaded the last of the files and quickly sent off an email letting her client know the final design was ready for review.

Finishing her breakfast, she drank a tall glass of water and got ready to take a walk. The gym was too expensive, obviously, but she'd taken to walking around the neighborhood for exercise. It was relatively safe with other townhouses and people around. She always switched up what time she went on a walk—mornings, afternoons, and early evening. She didn't want anyone to see her and notice any sort of routine.

Not that she suspected anyone was watching her, but it was always better to be safe than sorry. Grabbing her keys, she hurried out her front door. Blake was just climbing into his SUV. She nodded hello and wondered why he was leaving so late. Usually, he was out the door at the crack of dawn.

"Hey, Taryn!" Clarissa called out.

She nearly jumped in surprise but turned toward their front door. "Hi! Good morning."

Clarissa blew Blake a kiss but then crossed over to her. "I'm glad you could come by last night. I've been wanting to invite you over but things were so crazy with moving and trying to get settled here, I just hadn't gotten a chance yet."

"Yeah, the dinner was fun. Thanks again for inviting me. The food was all amazing, and it was nice getting to know a few people."

"Jackson seemed really taken with you."

"Oh, well, I don't really date," Taryn said, feeling flustered. A warm feeling coiled in her belly though, despite her admission. If she did date, Jackson was the type of man she'd be interested in. He was big enough to protect her but oddly seemed gentle under that tough exterior. He hadn't tried anything last night, hadn't sat too close to her or touched her in a way that made her uncomfortable. He was almost disconcertingly aware that she'd been nervous and had tried to put her at ease.

That didn't mean she was about to fall head over heels for the man though.

He was handsome and polite. Protective even. She couldn't get involved with anyone and certainly didn't want to drag him into her disaster of a life.

Clarissa backtracked when she saw Taryn was uncomfortable. "Sorry, I didn't mean anything by it or to butt into your life. He's quieter than the other guys but said he enjoyed talking with you."

"He was different than the others. Some of them seemed like a handful."

Clarissa laughed. "For sure. That's why they're still single. Jackson's a few years older like Blake though. He's not running around chasing after every woman he sees."

"How old is he?"

"Thirty-one. The same as Blake. Some of the younger guys are still in their twenties and sowing their wild oats, so to speak. I just meant he's a good guy if you were interested, but no pressure, obviously. I didn't mean to assume you were looking to date anyone. Do you want to grab breakfast? I've got online lectures later this evening that I need to prepare for but have the morning off."

"That must be nice."

"The schedule?"

Taryn nodded.

"Yeah, sort of. I'm used to getting to campus early and having lectures throughout the day, but because I'm teaching online this semester, I mostly have evening classes. It's totally different than anything I've done in the past. The time zone difference complicates things a bit, too. So what do you say about breakfast?"

"Thanks, but maybe another time," Taryn said. "I just ate. I'm headed for a walk around the neighborhood." That and she knew she couldn't afford wherever Clarissa wanted to go. She only had a few dollars to her name at the moment.

"I might run out to the store then. I had a craving for an omelet this morning. Blake didn't want to eat a big meal before PT, and then I realized we were almost out of eggs."

Taryn nodded, not wanting to tell her neighbor how little food she had at her own house. She'd be shocked, probably. She may have some design clients, but she was barely scraping by. Renting a huge townhouse was obviously a mistake, but she figured Austin would be more likely to look for her in a rundown apartment complex if he ever tracked her here. He certainly wouldn't check townhomes full of families and couples.

"I thought Blake usually left earlier in the morning," Taryn commented, wanting to change the subject.

"He does. They've got evening training later on, so he headed in a little late today. He probably won't be home until I'm done with my lectures tonight. Oh, do you want to come over for an early dinner? I've got a class starting at six-thirty."

"Thanks, but I wouldn't want to impose. I just came over last night for the barbeque."

"It's no imposition," Clarissa said with a smile. "We've got tons of leftover food—much more than we can finish on our own."

"Well, okay, if you're sure it's no problem."

"Trust me, it's not. Even with a hungry SEAL team, we ended up with way more food than I expected. Does five sound good?"

"Yeah, that's perfect. I don't mind eating earlier and will head out before your class."

"Awesome. I'll see you later on then."

Clarissa waved goodbye before walking back to her townhouse, and Taryn glanced back once more before going on her walk. It would be nice to have a friend here, she supposed. As long as Clarissa didn't push her to date Jackson. She didn't seem like the matchmaker sort, but one thing was for certain—she couldn't be in a relationship.

Taryn had to keep her head down and go about her life, not letting anyone find out too much about her past. Keeping a low profile was the only way to make sure her ex-husband never found her.

***

Jackson dropped to the ground after he'd rappelled down the wall, stepping back to watch his teammates come over one at a time. They drilled constantly for their missions—on the water, on land, in hand-to-hand combat.

The sun was beginning to set, obscuring their line

of site as they moved through the training course. He squinted as he looked up, watching Ethan swing his legs over before rappelling down. After this, they'd complete the course while being timed, trying to shave precious seconds off their performance from several weeks ago. When dealing with unknown enemies, being quick and moving forward without hesitation was imperative. They didn't have time to mull over options when they were moving in. They needed to charge forward as one unit, and drills like this kept their skills sharp.

On their last op to the Middle East, they'd captured a terrorist wanted for killing American soldiers in and around Bagram Airfield. They'd gone there twice after the asshole. The first time he'd slipped through their fingers, but the second time he hadn't been able to escape.

"Think we'll head back to Afghanistan soon?" Ethan asked, dropping down beside Jackson.

"As soon as we have intel on the missing Americans," he said with a frown.

Grayson came over the wall next and joined them, taking a swig of water from his canteen. "Hailey still has nightmares about the bombing. And she's worried sick over her friend Kim."

Jackson clenched his jaw. The two American women being held hostage concerned all of them. If they knew their location, they'd have staged a rescue the last time they were there. As it was, the two women were believed to be held in the mountainous regions of Afghanistan. No one had the exact coordinates. No one knew their condition. Had they been hurt? Raped? Killed?

Jackson's blood boiled at the idea of harm coming

to any women.

Troy jumped down next, moving quickly aside as Logan was hot on his heels. Their team leader, Blake, was the last man down, but he'd been watching from his perch at the top, ready to quickly descend.

"We'll start at the front of the course in five minutes," he said. "If our time is good, we can head home for the night. Tomorrow we've got another set of drills starting at oh-eight-hundred. We'll meet for regular PT beforehand."

The men began walking back to the front of the training area, talking amongst themselves. "Any word from the CO on the hostages?" Grayson asked Blake. They'd all briefed with their commander that morning, but Jackson knew he'd be eager for any new information. Even if Grayson couldn't tell Hailey any details personally because it was so highly classified, it was possible she'd learn something due to her work at the Department of Defense.

Hailey's friend Kim was an Army reservist and DOD contractor. No doubt Hailey would be informed to some extent if they had new intelligence—both because of her own position and because she'd been there at the time of the explosion.

"Not yet," Blake said. "As soon as we get a specific location, our team will be sent in for a rescue op."

"Damn it," Troy said, spitting on the ground. "It's not right to leave them over there."

"Agreed. But we'll waste time and resources running around if we don't know for sure where they are. They're gathering new intelligence daily. As soon as it's confirmed, we'll move in."

Ethan grumbled from beside Jackson. "Those

assholes will fucking pay for harming innocent women."

The other men glanced over at him. His eyes were heated as he looked at his teammates. "Hailey told me a little about Kim," he said in a low voice.

Grayson nodded. "Yeah, she mentioned that to me. She's worried as anything about her."

"She's in the reserves, but she's a contractor. She's not as highly trained as the other soldiers stationed there—I don't mean that in a negative sense, but it's true. She's not a career solider. She's got to be scared out of her mind. Fucking hell," he spat out, shaking his head. "Those women didn't deserve to be kidnapped by insurgents."

An officer on base barked out a command from the distance, and Blake looked at his teammates. "Two minutes," Blake said as they stopped at the front of the obstacles set up for training.

Some of the men took swigs of water from their canteens. Jackson's stomach rumbled, but he'd grab dinner after he got home. It had been a long day, and he was ready to complete the timed training and finish this up. They'd be back here drilling tomorrow morning soon enough.

Blake turned to him as they stood off to the side of the others. "Did everything go okay when you walked Taryn home last night?"

Jackson nodded. "Yeah. She's easily spooked though."

"I figured. I saw her when I was leaving this morning, and she nearly jumped out of her skin when Clarissa called out hello."

Jackson frowned, not liking the sound of that. She'd been startled by him yesterday, but he was a big guy. She knew her neighbor, and Clarissa wasn't the type of woman to intimidate anyone. He wished there was a way to make Taryn feel safe, but damn. If she was running from her ex-husband, the only thing to ease her fears would be for the asshole to end up behind bars.

"Is she in some sort of trouble?" Blake asked.

"Sort of. She ran from her ex," he said in a low voice. "I got the impression that she just up and left. She briefly panicked when I walked her home last night and a cop car drove by, but the asshole doesn't even live around here."

Blake stilled. "He's a cop? Was he abusive?"

Jackson could see the anger in his eyes. His teammates protected the innocent. They didn't tolerate men harming anyone weaker than them. They'd rescued women and children in all sorts of horrible situations around the world. They'd seen things that would give anyone nightmares. Taryn had been harmed on U.S. soil though, by a man who should've loved her. Who'd sworn an oath to protect others as a police officer. For Taryn to be betrayed by a man who'd promised to honor and protect her and who others looked to for help wasn't something they'd easily forgive.

"I'm still learning the details, but yes. She's afraid of her ex-husband. She was terrified just thinking it was him. She didn't tell me much though. I was there and saw her reaction. She ran, and I'm assuming she's afraid he'll track her down."

"Fuck," Blake muttered. "No wonder she's so skittish around men."

Jackson hardened. "She is, and I'm not sure what I can do to help her. I can't push for more information.

I barely even know her, but I swear if I find out that asshole's name, I'm tracking him down."

"She trusts you," Blake commented.

Jackson raised his eyebrows.

"She let you walk her back last night. She moved in a month ago and has barely talked to Clarissa or me. You sat there in my living room and ate dinner with her. She spoke more to you in an hour than she has to us the entire time she's lived next door."

"Maybe so, but that doesn't mean she'll spill her guts and tell me everything. I don't know where she's from. I don't even know if Taryn's her real name."

"Probably not," Blake agreed. "Not if she's smart. I'll keep an eye out for anything. I might have to let Clarissa know about this, too. If that asshole somehow finds Taryn, I don't want either of them to be in danger."

"Understood," Jackson said.

The other men gathered around them, and Blake told everyone to get ready. The sun sank lower in the sky, and Jackson wondered what Taryn was doing at that very moment. He was planning to stop by Raptor's house to look for the cell phone he'd inadvertently left there last night, but he couldn't just knock on Taryn's door, could he?

He didn't have a right to check up on her, and she might not appreciate the intrusion. One way or another, he wanted to find out more about her though. To make sure she was safe. It had been a long time since a woman had got under his skin, but something about her called to him. She sent his protective instincts soaring, and Jackson knew he wouldn't rest until he could ensure her complete and total safety.

Chapter 5

Taryn checked her email again that evening before she headed to Clarissa's. The client had finally approved her website changes and been thrilled with her redesign. She'd send them an invoice for the completed project but probably wouldn't get paid until tomorrow at the earliest.

Groaning, she closed her laptop.

Last week, she thought she'd found another new company to do some design work for, which would've given her another steady income stream, but they were unwilling to pay her off the books. Maybe she needed to look into getting a fake ID. With a new driver's license and new social security number, she could take more jobs. Pay taxes. Live a real life.

But how exactly would she get a new social security number?

Damn Austin for ruining her life. They'd married young when she'd found out she was pregnant, but a miscarriage in her first trimester had been both a blessing and a curse. She'd love to have a child and had cried her eyes out at the loss, but a child with Austin?

She was safer not being pregnant and not raising a child with him.

She'd stayed with him an entire year, but what had previously been harsh words and an occasional push or shove had gradually turned more and more violent. He'd slapped her across the face once, and it had only escalated from there. He'd hurt her. Bruised her. Locked her in their bedroom. Taken away her cell phone and laptop.

Austin controlled their finances, controlled their household and bills. She had a job, but he deposited the money into his bank account. She'd realized after they married that the joint account he'd reluctantly agreed to open with her had virtually nothing in it.

She'd hidden some money, biding her time, and when he'd finally snapped and thrown her into the wall of their house, she'd filed for divorce. It had been a long, drawn-out process, but he still followed her. Stalked her even when she'd tried to return to school.

She'd left everything when he'd shown up drunk one night and threatened to kill her. She'd taken a single bag and simply run.

Shuddering, she looked around her kitchen. She loved to work here where it was sunny and open and she felt safe. No one could hurt her here. Austin wasn't nearby. But the trauma seemed to stay with her, popping up at unexpected times. She liked the light and openness of her kitchen, the ability to sit there at the table and create. To not worry about him storming in, mad about some absurd thing.

And now because she was hiding and didn't have a secure, full-time position, she had to go another day without grocery shopping. She still had a small amount of peanut butter left in the jar and a few things in her fridge, but after paying her rent at the beginning of the month, she was left with next to nothing for food.

She should've gotten a roommate, should've rented a cheap apartment. She should've done a lot of things differently. Having a townhouse made her feel safer though. There were multiple ways to escape—the front door, the deck, the garage, and all the windows. If she stayed in a small apartment, she'd be trapped. And Austin wouldn't look for her here.

If he ever did manage to track her to San Diego, he'd look in apartments and other inexpensive housing. He'd probably look places that were popular with the college kids. She couldn't afford this place, and he'd know that. She'd already burned through the meager savings she had to afford rent. If she could just get more clients and take more jobs, she'd be okay. She had the skills, just not the freedom to take a position like that.

Her safety was the most important thing.

Austin could never, ever find her.

Sighing, she stood up from the kitchen table. Thankfully, Clarissa had invited her over. Taryn had skipped lunch and was starving. The meager breakfast she'd eaten hadn't done much to keep her full either. Maybe she should've skipped that long walk, but she liked getting exercise.

A few minutes later, she knocked on Clarissa and Blake's front door. His SUV was gone, and she assumed he was probably still on base training.

Was Jackson with him, she wondered?

No matter.

He'd already seen too much yesterday. She didn't need to drag a guy like Jackson into her complicated life or problems. He was older than her and had his job to worry about. An actual career. She was barely making ends meet and couldn't get a real job if she wanted to.

"Hi!" Clarissa said as she pulled open the front door.

"Hi. Sorry I'm a few minutes late. I know you have class later on."

"It's no problem," Clarissa assured her. "It's just leftovers, remember? I just took stuff out of the fridge. Make yourself a plate, and we'll reheat it in the microwave."

"All right, that sounds perfect," she said, following Clarissa inside. It was quiet, nothing like the boisterous group that had been there last night. Walking into the kitchen, she was surprised to see bridal magazines scattered around.

"I figured I better start planning," Clarissa said. "We'll probably get married next summer."

"Wow. Congratulations! Jackson did mention that the party last night was for your engagement, but no one was talking about it much, so I forgot to say something."

"It's fine. We're pretty low-key about it. I think the guys figured it out before we even made it official," she admitted with a laugh. "We'll probably just do a beach wedding here. Blake said we could have the wedding in Texas, but honestly, I didn't have a ton of close friends there. Blake's teammates are here, and I love the idea of a wedding near the ocean." She shrugged. "We'll figure it out."

Taryn absently nodded, putting some food onto a plate. There were indeed a large number of leftover platters of food. Her stomach rumbled, and she flushed, hoping her friend hadn't heard.

"Would you like a glass of wine?" Clarissa asked. "I'll pass since I'm lecturing tonight, but we have plenty."

"Water is fine," Taryn assured her. "So do Blake and his team usually have to work late?"

She wondered what the schedules of the SEALs were like. Not that anything would come of her and Jackson, of course, but she had to admit she was curious. The guys were all in perfect shape and clearly trained hard for their jobs. Even last night when they were all hanging out together, she could see how muscular and fit the men were. They might have been casual and having fun, but no doubt they could charge into any situation and take control if needed.

"It varies a lot," Clarissa said. "They do PT every morning but sometimes have evening or night drills. When they get sent on missions they could be gone for days or even weeks. Blake hasn't been gone much since I met him, but our relationship is pretty new. It sounds like it's unusual for them to be around so much."

"And you're already engaged?" Taryn asked before quickly hurrying on. "Sorry, I didn't mean that as a negative. It's just Jackson said you met over the summer."

"We did. It was fast, but we both just knew. It's hard to explain. I felt safe and at home when I was with him. I up and left everything in Texas. At first, I just came with plans to stay for the summer and see what happened, but we both quickly realized it was more."

"Wow. That's exciting though—a new life, new home, a marriage."

"Scary too, because of their line of work. What if something happens to him, you know? But I trust Blake and his teammates, so when he's out late for training or meets up with the guys for early PT, I know it's so he'll be safe when he's gone. I guess it's a little lonely since I just moved here and didn't know many people, but now that classes have started, I'll be busy again."

The women finished eating, talking a little about San Diego, and Taryn only shared a few small details about her own life. After cleaning up, she went home to let Clarissa get ready for her evening class. She was surprised when her friend knocked on her front door not even thirty minutes later, but it turned out her computer had frozen up and she needed help.

A few minutes later, Taryn sat in Clarissa's makeshift office, watching as she rebooted her laptop. "I'm so sorry for running back over to get you," Clarissa said, sifting through her papers as they waited. "It totally froze up when I tried to display the slides, and now I can't even get back online."

"Trust me, it happens all the time in my online classes," Taryn assured her. "After your laptop reboots, I'll show you how to share your screen with the students. They'll see the slides and be able to continue following while you talk."

"Geez, I can't believe how frazzled I am over this," Clarissa said, impatiently tapping her fingers.

"Could you teach out here?" Taryn asked. "Maybe

you could find a similar position at a university here in California so you could lecture in person again."

"I'm hoping to eventually find something. I haven't even looked into it yet. I wasn't ready to up and leave my job before, but now that Blake and I are engaged, things are different. We'll be here permanently, or at least until the Navy transfers him."

"Hmmm," Taryn said, frowning.

"What's wrong?"

"Oh, nothing. Just thinking."

Clarissa chuckled. "You're opposed to marriage? Or to marrying a Navy guy?"

Taryn shifted, looking at her neighbor. God, the last thing she wanted to do was admit she'd been married. And clearly Blake was nothing like her abusive ex. Clarissa was a smart, intelligent woman. She'd probably never understand how Taryn had ended up marrying an abuser. "Neither. I just can't imagine feeling settled like that—willingly giving up your career and home. You seem so happy."

"I am. And honestly, I wasn't that connected to things in Texas. I didn't have close friends or family there. I'm still teaching, just differently than before. It'll happen for you someday," Clarissa said. "You're young. You'll date, find a nice guy, eventually settle down…."

"Oh, it looks like your computer's back up," Taryn said, happy to change the subject. She watched as Clarissa logged in and clicked back to the link for her online class.

"Thank goodness it's working. Just show me how to display the slideshow, and I'll get back to my lecture. Somehow that's what messed me up earlier. I hope the students are still there."

"They will be," Taryn assured her. "It hasn't really been that long since you ran over to get me. Everyone has technical problems at some point with remote learning."

Taryn stepped off to the side so she wouldn't appear on camera, then pointed to where Clarissa needed to click. Mouthing "thank you" to her as the slides popped up on the screen, Clarissa apologized to the class and then continued on with the lecture.

Taryn silently slipped out the office door, leaving it cracked. It was only eight at night but already growing dark. The days were getting shorter this time of year, and she wondered what winters on the west coast would be like. She'd moved here without thought or research. And who was she kidding? She hadn't just moved. She'd run.

One small suitcase was all she'd brought with her, along with the cash she'd stashed when she'd still been married to Austin. She had her purse and her laptop, but that was basically it.

Taryn heard a car door shut outside and figured Blake had just gotten home. She nearly tripped over her own two feet as she saw both him and Jackson coming in the front door. Both men still had their fatigues on, and she tried to keep her jaw from dropping when Jackson's dark brown gaze locked with hers.

"Hey Taryn," Blake said. "I thought Clarissa had a lecture tonight."

"She does," Taryn said, flushing as she walked downstairs to the main level of the townhouse. Jackson's eyes were boring into her, and even though she had on jeans and a tank top, she felt practically naked with the way his gaze raked over her. It was possessive and somewhat protective all the same—like she was his to watch over.

Her pulse pounded, and she tried not to let her nerves get the best of her. She wasn't scared of Jackson. She was attracted to him. It was a little bit mind-boggling to feel attracted to a man again. She thought Austin had turned her off to dating and marriage forever. And it's not like she planned to marry Jackson. Goodness. She wouldn't even date him.

She just felt safe and somewhat flustered by the fact that he was here.

She nodded hello to him but continued talking. "Clarissa got kicked off her meeting and couldn't figure out how to stream her slides. She just ran next door to get me since I take online classes. Luckily I was able to help her."

"She's all set now?" Blake asked, frowning.

"Yep. I was just going to let myself out."

The two men exchanged a glance. "I'll walk you back," Jackson said, his voice gruff.

"Oh, uh, thanks."

"Is there any food left?" Blake asked, dropping his gear to the ground. "We haven't eaten yet, and I'm starving. We've been conducting training drills for hours."

"There's tons of food," Taryn said. "Clarissa invited me over earlier for dinner."

"She mentioned that. Jackson, I'll look around for your cell phone. It's bound to be here somewhere."

"Appreciate it. I didn't realize until I got home last night that I'd left it here." He gestured for Taryn to go ahead, and then they were both walking out of Blake's front door. A sense of déjà vu washed over her. They'd just done this exact thing last night. Except now Jackson was in his fatigues, looking gruff and sexy beside her. She didn't know what kind of drills they'd been doing all day, but it seemed like he'd just showered on base and put on a clean camo uniform. He smelled of clean soap, and with his large presence at her side, she didn't feel as jumpy as she usually did if she went outside at night.

Taryn almost wished her ex was in fact here to see her with Jackson at her side. She felt invincible beside him. He'd protect her if Austin ever showed up. Goodness. Austin probably wouldn't dare even show his face if Jackson was around. He liked tormenting her, but a man as big as Jackson? Austin would probably cower in the corner rather than come to blows with him.

Her skin prickled with awareness as Jackson shifted closer to her when a car passed by. It didn't even slow down, but she realized he was remembering her reaction from last night and trying to make her feel safe.

Her heart fluttered.

Jackson was a big, tough guy, but he seemed chivalrous, too. Without her even asking, he was watching out for her. He'd offered to walk her back. He was ready to protect her from danger.

She felt a little silly being so nervous all the time, but it wasn't from anything he'd said or done. Jackson didn't make a big deal about it. He just seemed to have a natural protective instinct.

"I think I can fix your trashcan," Jackson said, looking at it sitting up by her garage. It had been relatively easy for her to pull it back up the driveway that morning when it was empty. "I'll pick up an extra wheel next time I'm at the home improvement store. I need to get a few things for my place."

"Do you have a house?"

"No, just an apartment. I've got to put up some shelving though, so I'm planning to swing by the store when I get a day off."

"I should've left some lights on," Taryn said with a frown as they walked up her front steps. The porch light was on, but her house was completely dark. She'd rushed over to help Clarissa get back online for her class without even thinking about the lights. And now the sun had set, and she'd be entering her dark house alone.

"I'll go in with you," Jackson said, seeming to sense her unease.

She didn't comment, just unlocked the front door. Jackson moved in ahead of her to switch on the foyer light, and she realized with disdain that she still hadn't changed the bulb.

"It needs a new lightbulb."

"Do you have any? I'm tall enough to reach the light fixture without a ladder if I stand on the stairs. I can change it for you while I'm here."

"Yeah, thanks. I'll go grab one from the kitchen."

She had a new package of lightbulbs on the counter and cringed as Jackson led the way upstairs. She knew he was walking ahead of her because it was dark, but she didn't want him looking around her kitchen, realizing she barely had anything in it. She hardly had any furnishings or belongings at all. And she knew he took in everything as he flipped on another light and his gaze swept her living room.

"You keep the place clean," he commented as he turned toward the kitchen and flipped on another light.

"I don't have much," she said softly. Her laptop sat there on the kitchen table where she'd left it earlier, but she didn't have decorations or knick-knacks lying around. She didn't have pictures on her walls. Goodness. She didn't even have dirty dishes piled up. She barely had enough food to eat. "I bought some new lightbulbs last week," she said, gesturing toward the counter.

Embarrassment washed over her. Her nearly empty box of cereal was sitting there, along with the remains of her jar of peanut butter and a nearly empty sleeve of crackers. She hadn't bothered putting them away. Her cupboards were equally bare.

Not that he'd go snooping through them.

"I'd offer you something to eat, but I haven't gotten to the store yet."

He raised his eyebrows.

She met his gaze and froze. She'd been trying to make light of the situation, but in that instant, it felt like he could see straight through her—right into her very soul. Did he know how scared she was half the time? How she was barely keeping it together?

Had Jackson guessed that she hadn't gone to the grocery store yet because she was down to her last few dollars? Or did he think she'd just been busy?

"Uh, I'm planning to go tomorrow."

He didn't say anything for a moment but then grabbed the package on the counter. "I'll go change your lightbulb."

He disappeared, and Taryn let out a breath she hadn't even realized she'd been holding. Although he hadn't said anything, he clearly realized she didn't have much. An old sofa sat in her living room along with an inexpensive coffee table, but she didn't have a TV. She didn't have anything in her dining room. She'd gotten the small wooden table in her kitchen along with the matching chairs off a yard sale site. They were decent enough but clearly not brand new.

She had absolutely nothing in her basement.

Jackson appeared a moment later, holding the burned-out lightbulb. "All fixed."

"Thanks."

A beat passed, but Jackson didn't move from her kitchen. She wasn't sure what to do or even what to say. She hadn't invited anyone inside before, but Jackson clearly saw everything. He'd seen enough last night when she'd frozen in fear, whether she'd meant to reveal anything to him or not.

Now he saw her practically empty kitchen. Her sparse furnishings. The nicest thing she had was her laptop. She didn't dare admit to him that she'd been using the neighbor's wifi. She had to pay her own electricity and water bills. She didn't have a phone. She didn't have cable.

Jackson was competent and capable. He probably didn't know what to make of her situation, but it clearly bothered him.

"Listen, I know you just moved here without much," he said in a low voice. He set the burned-out lightbulb down on her table, and her gaze focused on his muscular hands. He was calm and collected, and she felt like she was about to fall apart. "You're still getting settled, and last night you admitted that you were scared of your ex-husband. You came here without anything, right?"

"I'll be okay," she said, her voice only wavering slightly. She swallowed, and she swore his face softened. Jackson, this big, tough Navy SEAL, who could probably kill a man with his bare hands, was trying to be gentle with her.

"You will be, but I'd like to help you out." He held up a hand as she started to protest. "I know you already ate dinner with Clarissa, so I can't very well take you out for a meal. Let me buy you some groceries for the week—just to help you get on your feet. You've been here a month or so, right? I'm sure you have bills and your rent to pay. Let me help you get started out on the right foot."

"Jackson, I couldn't let you do that," she said softly. "You can't pay for my groceries."

He shrugged. "I could offer to take you out to a nice dinner Friday night. We could go to a fancy steakhouse and easily spend what a week's worth of groceries cost. You wouldn't object to that, right? Just my doing this for you even if it costs the same amount?"

"Well…that's different."

"It is, but that doesn't mean I don't want to do it. Hell, I'd love to take you out to a nice dinner if I thought you'd ever agree to it."

"I don't date. I can't," she hastily added.

"I know, and I respect that. I can see that you're still scared of your ex, and I swear that I'd never hurt you. Taryn, I'd never lay a hand on you," he said, his eyes wide with sincerity as he looked at her. "I can't just stand by and let you starve though."

"I'm not starving," she said, her cheeks pinkening. "I just invoiced my client today and should get paid tomorrow."

"Should. I've got a steady paycheck thanks to the U.S. Navy. I've got money saved up. Hell, I get hazard duty pay for all my deployments to dangerous countries around the world. I can afford to buy you groceries for the week, sweetheart. Save the money you'll get from your client for an emergency. Please."

"Jackson," she said, her eyes watering.

"Taryn," he countered, his voice gruff. Her name on his lips did funny things to her insides. It was deep and commanding but comforting all the same. He was standing across the kitchen in his fatigues like a real-life G.I. Joe or something. He'd fight the bad guys and slay all her demons if she wanted. She couldn't let him do that for her though. Not when she had nothing to offer him in return.

A few tears slid down her cheeks, and she hastily wiped them away. She'd been trying so hard for the past month to survive. To get by with what little she had. Her neighbors hadn't seemed to notice she was struggling. How had Jackson, a man she'd just met, seen right through her?

"I didn't mean to make you cry," he said huskily.

"I just don't feel right about taking money from you."

"Then let me go pick up some groceries for you. I won't show you the receipt. It would help if you told me what you like though. Do you have any food in your fridge at all?" he asked.

"Just a few things," she whispered.

He nodded as if he'd suspected that all along.

Someone knocking on her front door had her jumping in fright. Jackson clenched his jaw, clearly not liking her reaction, but he attempted to soothe her. "That's probably Raptor. I left my cell phone at his place last night. I'll be right back."

She nodded, swiping away the tears on her cheeks.

She didn't like the fact that Jackson had to go answer her door, but what was she supposed to do? She didn't want Blake to see her standing there crying. She was afraid to answer the door alone anyway. She heard male voices talking, and then Jackson was closing her front door and coming back up the stairs.

Oddly enough, she felt comfortable with him here. She was embarrassed about her lack of money, but a man his size could easily overpower her. Hurt her.

She hadn't worried about that at all since he'd come inside. If anything, it was the opposite. She felt safer with him here. It was as if her topsy-turvy world had been righted. Just looking at him soothed something deep inside of her. She couldn't even explain it if she tried.

"I got it," he said, holding up his cell before pocketing it. "Raptor invited me over for some food, but I told him I was helping you out with a few things here."

"Aren't you hungry?" she asked.

His lips quirked. "Starving. How about I order a pizza? Then we'll order groceries online for delivery. I'll pay for it," he insisted. "And I'll set it up so if you need groceries again, you can order with my credit card."

"Jackson," she protested. "You can't just pay for my food."

"I can, and I will," he said, his voice gruff. "And don't worry—I don't expect anything in return. I'll admit that I'm attracted to you. Hell, I'd be a fool not to be, but I understand you're not in a place to date right now or feel comfortable yet around another man."

"I just—I've been so scared," she said, a few more

71

tears slipping down her cheeks. Helplessly, she swiped them away as she looked at him from across the room. "I ran from my ex-husband. Even though we were divorced by then, he was still following me. Waiting outside my apartment. Trying to hurt me. He won't ever leave me alone!" she sobbed, the tears falling harder now.

Jackson remained still but looked at her intensely. "Can I hold you?" he asked.

Her breath caught. She could tell him no, and he'd respect that. Jackson was an honorable man—the exact opposite of her ex-husband. He'd never force her, and he sure the hell wouldn't ever hit her or lock her in a room.

His arms represented safety, and at the moment, she craved that more than anything in the world.

She nodded, and then he crossed the kitchen toward her and pulled her into his muscular embrace. He was gentle, despite his strength, and she rested her head on his broad chest as the tears streamed down her cheeks. His camo fatigues were rough under her skin, but she wound her arms around him anyway, unwilling to let go. His muscular arms held her, and she felt safe for the first time in years.

Taryn shook in his arms, crying for all that she'd left behind and missed out on and for how hard her life had been. She couldn't see her family, couldn't see her friends. None of them knew where she'd run, and she wouldn't ever drag them into this. She was completely on her own.

Jackson's large hand ran over her hair, soothing her, and he ducked down. "Shhh," he whispered. "No one can hurt you here."

"I'm sorry," she babbled. "I didn't mean to cry all

over you and—" She choked out another sob.

"Don't ever be sorry for how you feel, sweetheart. I'm right here, and I'm not going anywhere. I'll never let anyone hurt you."

She wasn't sure how long they stood there in her kitchen, with Jackson's arms wrapped around her and her tears soaking his shirt. Finally, she pulled back, clutching onto his hand as she looked up at him. Her tears had finally stopped, and she was certain she looked awful, but there was nothing but concern in his eyes.

"Are you okay?"

She sniffed again but nodded. "We should order the pizza. You're hungry, and it's getting late."

"Sure thing. What kind do you like?"

"I already ate."

"I know, but I'm leaving you the leftovers for tomorrow."

Shakily, she took a step back from him. "Hawaiian is my favorite, but seriously, get whatever you want. I'll be happy with anything."

"Anchovies and onions?" he asked, his lips quirking.

She winced, and he chuckled. "I'm just teasing you. Hawaiian it is." He pulled his cell phone out of his back pocket and looked up the phone number for the pizza place nearby. "What's your house number? I know Raptor's is 126. Are you 124 or 128?"

"One twenty-eight."

He nodded and made the call, his deep voice making her stomach flip again. All he was doing was ordering a pizza. But no, it was more than that. He was taking control of the situation. Giving her a tiny bit of breathing room. He'd order food, and then they'd order groceries. She still felt guilty about that, but maybe he'd let her cook dinner for him sometime as a thank you. And for one week, she could relax just a fraction. Have a tiny amount of money in her bank account rather than only a couple of dollars. Go to bed without being hungry.

Maybe somehow, her life would eventually be okay after all.

Chapter 6

Jackson chuckled as he told Taryn some stories about his early days in the Navy. She'd seemed horrified by BUD/S, the grueling training men underwent to become SEALs. He loved seeing her smile though. Already, she was looking much more relaxed than yesterday.

She trusted him.

And that knowledge alone made him feel about ten feet tall.

Her cheeks were rosy and her eyes shining as she laughed and took another bite of the pizza. Even though she'd eaten earlier, she hadn't been able to resist a slice. And hell if he didn't enjoy providing for her. She wasn't his girlfriend—not now, and maybe not ever. Not if her ex had turned her off to relationships altogether. But Jackson decided then and there he'd do whatever it took to provide and care for her.

Things were different with Taryn—easy. He wasn't worried about what to say. He wasn't thinking about how to get her into bed. He was attracted to her, but he knew absolutely nothing would happen tonight. And that made it easy to just have a normal conversation with her.

Was this what it felt like for Raptor and Ghost when they met their girlfriends? Both of his teammates had seemed to instantly click with their women. One moment they were single, and the next? Each was involved in a serious relationship. Raptor and Clarissa were already engaged. Ghost had convinced Hailey to move in with him. And he'd never seen his buddies happier.

His lips quirked as Taryn's eyes met his, still sparkling in amusement. "I know you enjoy being a SEAL, but I have to be honest—that sounds awful."

"It was," he agreed. "They don't call it hell week for nothing."

"I'll stick with graphic design, thank you very much."

He chuckled. "Fair enough. So you have a few clients you do design work for?"

She nodded, looking a little nervous. "I do. I don't have a regular nine-to-five job—not anymore. I get paid off the books for my work. I ran from my ex-husband when I came here. I left everything behind."

"I know," he said, trying to look reassuring.

"I had to use a new name—a new identity." She paused a beat as she watched him. "Why don't you look surprised?"

Jackson lifted a shoulder. "You hesitated yesterday when I asked your name."

Her jaw dropped. "You knew I was lying?"

He shrugged. "Lying or nervous to tell me. I'll admit I appeared out of nowhere when I showed up at Raptor's house. I realize I'm a big guy."

"You're huge."

He chuckled as she blushed prettily. He was indeed well-endowed, but he didn't want her to worry about that. He knew she meant he was tall and muscular. He didn't know exactly how her ex-husband had treated her. Had he hurt her physically? Raped her? Abused her in other ways with harsh words and controlling behavior?

Taryn was a good foot shorter than him, and slender at that. If their relationship ever progressed to where they were intimate, he'd have to be careful. He'd always go at her pace and let Taryn call all the shots. And they weren't even in a relationship—they'd just met. And she'd already said she didn't date, so he shouldn't even be thinking about things like that.

"I know I can intimidate people," he said in a low voice. "It works to my advantage in the field. When we're taking down armed men or rescuing hostages, I can do what I need to do. I've got a huge advantage physically. I didn't like that I frightened you yesterday though."

She licked her lips, looking nervous. "My ex hurt me."

He stiffened. "Did you go to the police?"

"He was the police. We lived in a small town, and he was the golden boy. Everyone thought Austin could do no wrong." She gasped as her hands flew to her mouth. Apparently, she hadn't meant to let his name slip. That didn't mean Jackson wouldn't be looking into him. Looking him up. Calling in a few favors. He had military friends all over the world. It wouldn't end well for the asshole that had dared to harm Taryn. Even if she'd asked him to stay on the sidelines, Jackson knew he'd be tracking the motherfucker down. All he needed was a little more information.

"I didn't mean to tell you his name," she hastily said. "He can't ever find me here. Ever. I managed to divorce him, but he'll never let me go. He followed me back to where I'd attended college and threatened me again. He'll spend his life looking for me. And when he does?" Her voice shook, and Jackson's blood boiled.

"I can protect you." His voice was gruff, with a hard edge to it, and he tried to keep his face passive. He was livid. Furious that a man had so much as laid a finger on her with ill intent. And he could see she was genuinely terrified. Her ex had no doubt done horrible things to her.

Her gaze darted to the sliding glass doors leading to her deck as she wrung her hands in her lap. "I'm always paranoid he'll find me and break in somehow," she admitted. "I changed my name and moved across the country. I change my routine every day in case I'm being watched, but if he ever comes? Nothing will stop him."

Jackson's gaze slid to the glass doors. "You keep your doors and windows locked. I can put a wooden dowel in the bottom track to prevent anyone from sliding that open. It'd be hard to get up onto your deck though—there's no stairs leading to the ground."

"Not on mine, but my neighbors have a bigger deck with stairs. The neighbors on the other side of the house—not Blake's."

Jackson nodded, clenching his jaw. "I think your neighbors would notice a man on their deck or prowling around their backyard. And it would be hard as hell for him to track you here if you changed your name and aren't using your social security number for work."

"I can't. He'd find me—lie, steal information and files, whatever it took. I even dropped my old clients so I'd have a fresh start."

"But you can't get a decent job this way or save up any money. Sweetheart, you're barely scraping by. Are you sure you don't want to report him?"

"I can't. I'll just make do for now."

"Hell, I'd support you if you'd let me."

"No way," she interrupted.

He resisted the urge to smile. "I figured as much. And I admire and respect that you're taking classes online and working. Wouldn't you feel better to put this behind you though? To have him arrested and live a life on your own terms? You could work where you want, go where you want, and not be scared all the time."

"I can't, Jackson. I just can't. You don't know what he's capable of."

"What did he do to you?" he asked, his voice hard.

Taryn pressed her lips together and shook her head. His stomach clenched as he saw her hands shaking.

"Shit. I didn't mean to frighten you. It's just that it kills me to know there's a man out there that hurt you."

"Maybe someday I'll tell you, but not right now."

He nodded. He didn't like it, but he also wanted

her to trust him. He'd only known her for twenty-four hours. It wouldn't be fair for him to expect her to spill her entire life story to him. He wanted her to feel comfortable enough to tell him anything, but damn. He had the feeling that if he pushed too hard, she'd shut him out. She'd let him into her home, let him order her dinner and groceries. But letting him into her life and heart were entirely different things.

It was a miracle he was even sitting here with her right now.

"You moved into this neighborhood so he couldn't find you," Jackson ascertained.

She nodded. "He'd expect me to live in a cheap apartment or something. This is more than I can afford, but I'm hoping to get new clients so I'm not constantly struggling. If he ever tracks me to San Diego, he wouldn't start in a relatively well-off neighborhood like this."

"I'm guessing you wouldn't want to move in with me? No expectations," he quickly added. "I've got a two-bedroom apartment. You could have your own space and save up some money."

"Jackson, you're really sweet—"

"Sweet?" he asked, his eyebrows raising.

She flushed but smiled at him. "Don't worry, I won't tell your SEAL buddies."

He laughed out loud then, the sound echoing around her kitchen. Hell no, his teammates would never believe that. They'd never expect him to go soft over a woman. Then again, Raptor and Ghost had fallen hard. They'd kill for Clarissa and Hailey. And damn. If Taryn's ex ever showed up, he knew he'd do whatever was necessary to protect her, consequences be damned.

"So are you going to tell me your real name?" he asked gently.

She paused, and he could see the genuine fear in her eyes. She swallowed once and then surprised him by answering. "Tara. My real name is Tara. I didn't want something unrecognizable, and Taryn sounds similar enough, but if he searches for me, he'd look under my real name. I changed my middle and last name, too, of course."

"That's smart. If you won't go to the police, you're doing the best you can to stay hidden. To survive. That doesn't mean I don't hope you'll let me help you more though."

The doorbell rang, and Jackson rose. "That's probably the groceries. I'll get them and then let you put everything away and get situated. It's getting late, and I should head out soon. We've got PT bright and early in the morning."

"Okay, I didn't mean to keep you here so long," she apologized.

"It's no trouble," he assured her.

Jackson crossed her kitchen and went down into the foyer. She had a regular lock and chain, but he'd feel better adding a deadbolt as well. It would be harder for someone to break in. Mentally, he was already tallying a list of what he'd need at the hardware store. Maybe he could swing by after work one day and then knock off a few projects here over the weekend.

He took the grocery bags and carried them up to Taryn's kitchen. She was already putting away the leftover pizza, and his stomach clenched at how empty her fridge was. He'd already ordered more groceries than she'd needed, but he'd bring by a few more things, too—condiments, staples like butter and cooking oil. He'd ordered her plenty of food but hadn't considered she literally had nothing here.

"Jackson," she said in surprise, eyeing all the bags. "You ordered way too much."

He set the bags on the table, careful of her laptop. "I know you'll make good use of everything, and some of it is to stock your pantry. I thought maybe I could drop by this weekend—fix the wheel on the trashcan and then do a couple of things to make your home more secure."

"I'd appreciate it," she said gratefully. Jackson knew she wasn't someone who liked accepting help, but if it would make her safer, she'd do it. "Maybe I could fix you dinner or something," she added shyly.

His heart pounded. There was a faint flush across her cheeks, and male pride swelled in his chest. "I'd like that," he admitted. "And while I'm pretty handy with home repairs, I'm not much of a cook."

"Good. Well, Saturday then? Although I admit it's tough for me to accept help, I do appreciate that you're trying to make me feel safer here."

"You will be safer," he assured her. "And yep—Saturday works. There's always a chance we'll get called out on an op, but I expect to be here. If I had to leave for some reason, I'd make sure to let you know."

"Of course," she said. "I understand."

He nailed her with a gaze. "If you're ever in trouble though—serious trouble—I'd drop everything to get here for you."

"You barely even know me," she said softly.

"I want to get to know you. I can be patient, sweetheart. I'll be your friend and won't ever push you for anything. And even if we ever did get to the point where you'd let me date you, I still wouldn't force you to do something you don't want. Ever. You're the one in control here."

"I…I like you," she whispered.

"I like you, too."

She hesitated for a moment, looking innocent in the tank top and jeans she was wearing. Taryn was young, but she'd been through a hell of a lot. She crossed over and hugged him then, shocking the hell out of Jackson. He knew Taryn was weary, but her trust meant everything to him. "Be safe, Tara," he whispered in her ear. She stiffened, clinging to him. "I won't tell anyone your real name. That's for me alone," he said, his voice gravel.

"Okay," she whispered, stepping back. She clung to his shirt though, and Jackson ducked down, brushing his lips across her forehead. It was tender, and she closed her eyes at his touch. He'd love to pull her closer and kiss her for real, but now wasn't the time. She might never be ready for something like that. Taryn was scared and vulnerable, and he had to move slowly and be infinitely patient with her. He'd be her friend, and if anything else ever happened beyond that, he'd die a happy man.

"Do you have a cell phone?" he asked as he stepped back.

He frowned as she shook her head no. "Tell me your email address then. I need a way to reach you. And I'm getting you a phone for emergencies."

"Jackson, you can't do that!"

"I can, and I insist on it. You need for your safety if nothing else. I'll get a prepaid one with minutes already on it. You can save it for emergencies if you want, but this is something I can't take no for an answer on."

She hesitated but finally agreed. "I would feel safer with a phone. Now if I need help, I have to run next door to one of my neighbors' houses. And when I go and run errands, I don't have a way to call 911 in an emergency."

"I'd feel better if you had one, too," he admitted.

She gave him her email address, and he quickly sent her a message so she'd have his email as well. "Why don't we plan on two Saturday afternoon? I can get a few things done here, and then we can eat dinner if you're still up for it."

"Absolutely."

"All right then. Goodnight, Taryn. Stay safe for me, okay?"

"I'll be careful."

He nodded again then turned and crossed her kitchen. If he pulled her into his arms, he'd never want to leave. She followed him down the stairs to her foyer, and he looked back at her one last time. "Make sure you lock up. Use the chain, too."

"I will. And thanks for everything, Jackson."

He opened the front door and walked onto her porch, his chest clenching. The last thing he wanted to do was leave her. It was late though, and he'd been gone since this morning. He had his own things to attend to at his apartment, and he had to be up early for PT. He'd see her this weekend. He'd email her since she didn't have a phone to call or text.

Leaving Taryn was harder than he wanted to admit to himself though.

Chapter 7

Taryn fluttered around her townhouse on Saturday morning, her nerves rattling. Jackson was coming over again today. Jackson. The man who'd inadvertently scared her only a week ago. What if she hadn't been trying to lug her trashcan down the driveway right when he arrived at Blake's house? Would she never have met him?

She had a feeling she'd have missed out on a lot if that were the case. It was an odd thought, because she still hardly knew him. They'd exchanged a few emails, and she'd asked Clarissa a bit about him when they'd had coffee one afternoon.

They were still practically strangers though. She didn't know where he was originally from, or anything about his family, or what his favorite foods or drinks were.

She trusted him though. Unlike the uneasiness she'd always felt with Austin, Jackson made her feel safe. He was a large man who could easily overpower a woman, but she somehow knew he wouldn't harm her.

Goodness.

What if she hadn't run back over to help Clarissa the other night? Would she ever have seen Jackson again? He'd ended up at her house for a couple of hours that evening while they ate pizza, ordered groceries, and talked.

Was she crazy for letting him come over again?

Nervously, she looked around her kitchen again. She'd decided to make tacos for dinner and was already second guessing herself. What if Jackson didn't like Mexican? What if he wished they'd gotten carry-out instead?

Sighing, she took a deep breath, trying to calm her nerves.

She was acting like this was a date or something. He was just coming by to help her.

The doorbell rang, and she peeked out the front window. Clarissa stood on her porch holding a cell phone. Confused, Taryn went to the door. "It's Jackson," Clarissa said, grinning.

She winked and handed Taryn the phone, hurrying off to her own house before Taryn could say a word.

"Hello?"

"Hi sweetheart, it's Jackson," he said needlessly. No doubt he'd heard Clarissa a moment ago. "I called Clarissa's cell since you don't have a phone yet. Sorry about that, but I'm at the store right now and didn't have a good way to get in touch. I hope she didn't mind too much."

"She seemed to think it was funny," Taryn said, walking back inside her own house. "She was grinning from ear to ear."

"Now Raptor will probably be on my case about you," Jackson joked. "I told her I was getting you a new phone today. I already picked it up and am finishing up a couple of other errands right now. Do you need me to grab anything for when we eat later on?"

"I've got plenty of food thanks to you. I'm making tacos tonight, so I hope you like Mexican."

"I love it," he assured her.

"I don't have much in the way of drinks actually. If you want a beer or something, maybe you could bring a six-pack?"

"Sure thing. And what do you like? I can get stuff for margaritas. I know some of the other women like those."

"I love margaritas, but that's expensive to buy a whole bottle of tequila. And I wouldn't have more than a drink or two."

"It'll last," he assured her. "Didn't Clarissa want to have a girls' night sometime? You'll have extra ingredients for when you do."

"Well, okay, but only if you let me pay you for it."

"No way," he said with a chuckle. "I already offered to bring it. I'll grab the tequila, triple sec, and some limes. I got a few other things for you at the grocery store, too."

"Jackson, you can't keep buying me all this stuff."

"It's just until you get on your feet, sweetheart. I swear I don't mind. I like taking care of you," he added huskily.

Her heartbeat quickened, and she felt a flush creeping over her. It was flattering to have the attention of a man like Jackson. He was handsome, and when the man was in uniform? He probably left a trail of broken hearts everywhere he went.

She didn't know if he'd eventually expect more though. He said he was patient and would be her friend for now, but she had a feeling he'd eventually want more. Wasn't he flirting with her already by calling her sweetheart? He certainly didn't call his friends' girlfriends that.

How would she feel if he eventually started dating someone else? She'd have no claim on Jackson if she insisted they stay friends.

Were they just friends? She'd cried all over the man earlier this week as he'd held her in his arms.

"Are you still there?" he asked.

"Yeah, sorry, I was just thinking."

"About what?"

"This. Us. I'm worried you'll eventually want more than I give you."

"Hey," he said softly. "I'm not in a hurry. I like you, sweetheart. I know you've been through a lot. I'm not interested in any other women, so if you want to take things slowly and just let me be your friend for now, I'm okay with it."

"Do you buy all your female friends groceries and cell phones?"

"I don't have a lot of female friends," he admitted.

Flushing, she looked around her kitchen. "That's just it. I'm worried you'll start to expect more. We're more than friends Jackson, aren't we?"

"I care about you," he said in a low voice.

Taryn blew out a shaky breath. "We barely know one another."

"We'll get to know each other. I don't want you to worry. We'll just take things one day at a time. I'll come over and do a few things around your place this afternoon, we'll eat, and that's it. If you want to see me again after that or need me for something, I'll be there."

Taryn closed her eyes. She would want to see him again. She already knew that. As strange as it was, she felt safer with Jackson than without him. She didn't think she'd ever trust a man again, but something about him made her feel protected and secure.

Was she playing with fire though? Her brief marriage to Austin had turned her off to relationships. She trusted Jackson as her friend, but as for anything more?

"Taryn?" he asked softly when she didn't say anything.

"Okay," she finally said. "I'll stop freaking out."

He chuckled, and the low sound made her belly flip. She took another deep breath, trying to be braver than she felt. "I'll see you around two?"

"I'll be there."

They ended the call, and she rustled around her kitchen again. She had ground beef, cheese, and homemade salsa that she'd already prepared. Fortunately, she'd gotten paid earlier in the week, so she'd picked up some extras at the grocery store. Normally she relied on basics to get by, trying to stretch her dollar, but she wanted to make a nice meal for Jackson. And it's not like she'd splurged on an expensive steak or something. He'd paid for a lot of the food himself when he ordered her groceries earlier in the week.

She straightened up a bit around her living room and then realized she still had Clarissa's phone. She walked next door, and Blake answered when she rang the doorbell. He raised his eyebrows as Taryn held out the phone. "This is Clarissa's," she explained. "Jackson, um, called me since I don't have a phone yet."

Blake took the phone from her, smiling. "You and Jackson, huh?

She flushed as he chuckled. "He's a good guy, Taryn. I know you prefer to keep to yourself, but if you ever need anything, Clarissa and I are right next door. We're happy to help out."

She shifted uncomfortably, wondering how much Blake knew about her past. What had Jackson told him? "Thanks. I appreciate it. And I'm getting a cell phone, so you won't be getting any more of my calls."

"Have Jackson give you our numbers. I know you can easily come next door, but just in case of an emergency, it'd be good to be able to contact each other."

"I will. Thanks again."

She turned and hurried to her own house, surprised to see Jackson already pulling up. The morning had flown by though, and it really was already two in the afternoon. Blake nodded at his buddy but turned around, closing his front door.

Jackson parked in her driveway and climbed out of his SUV, his eyes warming as he looked at her. He had on jeans and a dark tee shirt, but it did little to conceal his muscles and strength. He hadn't shaved today, and the dark stubble on his jaw was sexy as hell.

Her heart fluttered just looking at him.

She was surprised to feel attracted to a man again. Her ex had left her fearful and more concerned about her safety than interested in any guy that she saw. But

Jackson was big and broad, with those dark brown eyes that seemed to see everything. The way he watched her intently made her feel safe. Nothing would jump out of the shadows to hurt her. Not when he was around.

"Hi, sweetheart," he said with a grin, and her stomach did a funny little flip. He opened the back hatch of his SUV and grabbed a bunch of bags. She rushed over to help him, but he immediately waved her off. "I got it."

"Wow. What is all that stuff?"

"I got a deadbolt for your front door, the wooden dowel for your deck, and a wheel to fix the trashcan. I was worried you might not have any tools. I know I could borrow some from Raptor, but I picked up a few basics for you as well."

"Jackson, wow—I won't be able to repay you for all this stuff."

"I don't expect you to," he said calmly. "Some of this is for my peace of mind, too. If you're here alone, I want to know that you're safe."

She nodded uncertainly, understanding to some extent what he meant. He'd feel better knowing she had a strong lock on her front door and some other items to make her house more secure. Jackson wasn't her boyfriend though. He shouldn't need to feel like it was his responsibility to take care of her.

What if he got frustrated with how little she had to offer him? She didn't want to sleep with him. She didn't have extra money for them to go out places together. She couldn't very well buy him anything since she was barely scraping by.

"What's wrong?" he asked in a low voice.

"I just feel guilty that you're doing all this for me."

"There's no reason to feel guilty. You're making me dinner, right?"

"Well, yes, but you basically paid for most of the food yourself."

"Like I said—I would've been happy to take you out to dinner one night. You don't want to date anyone now, and I respect that, but that would've involved my paying for dinner. Don't feel guilty just because we're going about things a little differently."

She relented, conceding he had a point before leading him toward her front door. Maybe she should be upset he'd taken control of a few things—he'd bought her a phone and household items. He'd paid for her groceries. Jackson was nothing like her abusive ex-husband though. He was taking care of her, with her safety and best interests in mind. He wasn't demanding anything from her.

They stopped on her front porch as she unlocked the front door. Even though she'd only gone over to Clarissa's to return the cell phone, that was one habit she'd never break.

She glanced back as Jackson's gaze locked with hers. "You look pretty," he said, his eyes warm as he looked at her. She smiled shyly up at him. She'd put on a sundress and sandals, feeling comfortable enough with Jackson to wear it around him. Her ex would've no doubt tried to stick his hands up her dress, claiming she was his to touch however he wanted.

Austin had always made her uncomfortable. Sure, his attention had been flattering on their first few dates, and she'd eventually let him take her to bed. Then she'd wound up pregnant. Married.

And after that?

He'd taken over her entire life. He was controlling. Mean. After they'd had a shotgun wedding because of the pregnancy, she'd seen his true colors, and she'd been scared whenever they were in the same room together.

"Are you okay?" Jackson asked softly.

Taryn realized she'd gotten lost in her own thoughts of the past once again. "I'm fine," she assured him. "Let's go inside."

He nodded, clearly not believing her, but he followed her in anyway. Jackson carried everything up to her kitchen, pulling out the food and handing her a six-pack of beer. "You're sure you're okay with my being here?" he asked after she'd put it into the fridge. "I don't want you to ever feel uncomfortable around me."

She looked over at him, hating the concern on his face. "I promise, I'm fine. I was thinking about my ex-husband when we were outside. It just scared me for a minute."

"I'd never hurt you," he said seriously.

She swallowed and then crossed the kitchen toward him, clutching onto his muscular forearm. She had to tilt her head back to look at him, so Jackson grabbed one of the kitchen chairs and sank down into it. He gently pulled her toward him, and tears filled her eyes.

"What is it, sweetheart?"

She clung to Jackson like he was her lifeline, willing him to see. "He hurt me. We got married because I was pregnant. He was always a bit controlling, but after I became his wife? He'd hit me. Lock me in the bedroom. Threaten that I could never see my friends or family again."

Jackson stiffened, and she could tell he was willing himself to stay in control. Jackson and his friends were the type of men that protected others—who risked their lives for their country. They might hurt the bad guys, but they protected those weaker than them.

She could tell he was angry about her past—angry at her ex-husband.

"I'm just telling you this so you'll understand. I don't want you to feel sorry for me or anything. Sometimes little things remind me of him, and I'm scared."

"Feel sorry for you? I want to fucking kill the bastard." Jackson's voice was calm, but she heard the steely undertone beneath it. This man was positively lethal.

"He completely controlled my life. Believe it or not, I'm a lot more comfortable in my own skin now, but I'm still scared a lot of the time. I'm afraid he'll find me."

"I understand your reluctance to go to the police given his job, but if you ever wanted to, I'd be right there at your side."

"No, I can't!"

"Shhhh," he soothed. She relaxed her grip on his forearm. "Have you ever gone to counseling?" he asked.

"I can't afford it. I don't have health insurance, and as you realized the other day, I'm barely scraping by."

Jackson took her hand, running his thumb gently over her knuckles. His touch was so soft and soothing, she wanted to throw herself into his arms and just let him hold her. To never let go. That

94

wouldn't be fair to Jackson though—not when she couldn't offer him a real relationship in return.

"I care about you, Taryn."

"This seems so fast though," she said, flustered. "I just met you last week."

"It's fast, but that doesn't make my feelings for you any less real."

"I like you, too, Jackson. I just feel like I can't offer you much. I mean—I literally don't have anything," she said, a few stray tears running down her cheeks as her voice wobbled.

"I don't need anything but you," he said, his voice husky. "I was drawn to you the moment I first saw you. Call it fate or whatever you want, but I feel like you were sent here to me."

He gently drew her even closer to him, giving her a chance to pull back or push him away. She knew if she told him to stop, he would. He'd get up and leave if she asked. She wanted the safety and comfort of his arms though. She wanted Jackson and all that he represented. He was gentle but strong. Honorable.

She trusted him.

Taryn let him ease her onto his lap as she softly cried. He didn't say anything, just ran his large hand over her hair. His lips were at her ear, soothing her. "You're safe with me, sweetheart. Never doubt that." She cried even harder.

She didn't know how long Jackson held her, but eventually her tears slowed.

"I need to stop crying every time you come over," she said, clutching onto his shirt. Jackson smelled of soap and something else woodsy, like pine. It was clean and fresh. Her ex-husband always wore an awful, gag-inducing cheap cologne. Jackson was raw and real.

"You will," he assured her. "You've been through a lot. You can let it all out around me."

Rather than resisting, she relaxed further into him. She'd felt alone ever since she'd run from her ex. She didn't have friends or family who knew where she was. She had nothing here in her townhouse. But for the first time, it felt like home. And she knew that had everything to do with Jackson.

Chapter 8

"Damn, that smells amazing," Jackson said as he walked into the kitchen a couple of hours later. Taryn was standing at the stove in her sundress, a breeze blowing in from her open balcony doors, and his chest hurt at how right the entire scene was.

He had an urge to go to her and pull her into his embrace, but knew he had to tread carefully. Taryn was wary of relationships, and if theirs had to be the slowest in history, he was okay with it. Call it whatever you wanted, but after the way he'd held her earlier, they were certainly more than just friends.

Taryn looked over at him, grinning. "I love to cook. Now that I have some spices and extras in the pantry, I'll be able to make a lot more dishes."

"Hell, tell me whatever you need, and I'll get it," he said with a chuckle. "Just as long as I'm invited over for dinner every once in a while." He winked, but her laughter let him know she realized he was teasing her.

Jackson stopped a few feet away from her, loving the look of happiness on her face. She turned down the burner and stepped back from the stove. "I'm going to let that cook ten more minutes, but then dinner will be ready. I made homemade salsa, too."

"I can barely cook anything," he admitted sheepishly. "I don't grill because I'm in an apartment."

"I don't grill because I don't have one or know how," she said with a shrug.

Jackson nodded toward the doors. "It's nice having the deck right here off your kitchen. Raptor's is off the living room."

"It's a different layout than my townhouse. I don't usually leave the doors open," she admitted. "I feel safer when you're here." She flushed at her admission, and Jackson's chest swelled with pride. He didn't like that she was nervous here alone, but to know that she felt safe with him? That meant everything.

"I understand why you're cautious," he said. "If you're right here in the kitchen though, you'd hear anyone who got on your deck. And like I said before, without stairs leading up to it, you shouldn't need to worry too much."

"Easier said than done," she said lightly.

"I added a deadbolt to your front door," Jackson said, pulling a set of keys from his pocket. He handed them to Taryn and swore sparks shot through him as their fingers brushed against one another. Her own hand was small and delicate. It looked fragile compared to his muscular, calloused hand.

Her cheeks were still pink as she set the keys on her kitchen counter. He wondered if she'd been as affected as him by their innocent touch.

"Thank you for adding it. I'll feel better having the extra lock on the house."

"No problem. And I know it's not really my business to keep making suggestions for your home, but have you thought about one of those video doorbells?"

"Yeah. I even asked the landlord if I could install one. They gave me the okay, but I'd have to pay for it myself." She glanced over and caught the look on his face. "And no, Jackson, you can't buy me one. You've done more than enough already—the cell phone, the deadbolt, the food. I seriously can't accept anything else."

He frowned but nodded, not wanting to make her uncomfortable. If he had his way, he'd rush out and buy one right now. He also wanted to know more about her ex. Taryn might not be ready to open up to him, but damn. He wanted to know everything he could about this guy. It sounded like she'd run clear across the country, and here she was, still scared in her own home.

"Do you want to make margaritas, or should I?" he asked.

"Are you having one, too?"

"I'm happy with a beer," he said with a low chuckle. "I'll make you one though since you're busy cooking."

"Not too strong," she said quickly.

"No problem," he said. He moved to her refrigerator, grabbing the limes he'd stuck in there earlier. Unlike the bare shelves she'd had a week ago, it was looking quite full at the moment. He'd ordered more groceries than she needed, but she'd gone and picked up a few small things as well.

Taryn stood at the stove, stirring the ground beef again. Something she'd said in passing earlier was weighing on him. Taryn had mentioned she'd married her ex because she'd been pregnant. She hadn't mentioned having a child though.

Had she had an abortion? Left her child behind? He couldn't imagine her doing that, and the fact that she hadn't mentioned being a mother made him question that scenario. Maybe something had happened to the baby. Jackson cleared his throat. "I don't mean to bring up bad memories, but you said earlier that you got married because you were pregnant."

She looked over at him, a sad expression on her face. "Yeah. I was, but I had a miscarriage in the first trimester. Crazy, huh? If we'd waited a few more months, I never would've married him. I found out pretty early on that I was pregnant. Austin swept me off my feet. At first, I thought he was everything I'd been looking for. I wasn't planning to get pregnant—we were careful—but when it happened? It seemed like the perfect step to take. We rushed down to the courthouse the following week."

"Damn," Jackson muttered.

"Yeah. It turns out it was the biggest mistake of my life."

"Did your family know you were married?"

"They did. He was charming and polite when they met. I mean, he was with me, too, when we first started dating. I'm not as much of an idiot as you probably think."

"I don't think you're an idiot."

"I was young and naïve. And they only met him

once. My parents and I aren't close, and they didn't know I was pregnant. I never told anyone about it or when I lost the baby. Austin ranted and raved about it." She shook her head.

"He was an asshole," Jackson muttered. "He is a complete asshole."

"Well, he only got worse after that," she said bitterly.

"I'm sorry."

"It's not your fault."

"No, but I'm sorry you had to deal with any of that. I'm sorry you had to run and leave your entire life behind."

She took a shaky breath, and Jackson's chest clenched. He wanted to get to know her better and help her, but maybe he shouldn't have brought that up. She'd probably tell him more in her own due time.

Jackson finished mixing her margarita and grabbed himself a beer. He was kicking himself for not bringing her a pitcher of some sort. He'd been so pleased with himself for bringing the ingredients, he'd forgotten she probably didn't have a lot of serving pieces in her kitchen.

He took a pull of his beer, watching her finish cooking. Her sundress swirled around her legs as she moved. He wouldn't say anything about it because he didn't want to freak her out, but it was sexy as hell. She had gorgeous, toned legs that he'd love to run his hands up. Nice hips. Full breasts.

He'd never touch her without her consent, but holy hell. Taryn was beautiful.

She left the ground beef in the pan she'd cooked it in but moved toward the fridge, pulling out the homemade salsa, shredded cheddar, and flour tortillas. "I'll quick warm these in a pan, and we'll be all set."

"How'd you make the salsa?" he asked.

"Tomatoes, jalapenos, salt, and a splash of lime juice. I've got cilantro to sprinkle on top since I wasn't sure if you liked it."

"Who doesn't like cilantro?" he quipped.

"Right?" she joked. "I don't usually buy fresh herbs, but I'll use this up since I love it."

He handed her the margarita, his lips quirking as she took a sip and smiled. "This is amazing. Where'd you learn to mix drinks like this?"

"I'm self-taught," he said with a wink. "And I'm thirty-one, so I've had plenty of years to perfect it."

"Hmmm."

"How old are you?" he asked, watching as she set her drink back down and continued warming the tortillas.

"Twenty-three."

"Does it bother you that I'm older than you?" he asked, genuinely interested. Some women Taryn's age were still quite immature—hanging out at bars every weekend, drinking with their friends. Taryn almost seemed like she'd lived a lifetime in her short years. She was independent and had established a career of sorts for herself. She'd dealt with a lot and was still pushing forward.

"Bother me? No. I feel safe with you, Jackson."

She glanced over at him, and his heart warmed. "I'm glad."

She shrugged, putting the tortillas onto a plate. "My husband was only a couple of years older than me, but he was a total asshole. He was chauvinistic and abusive. I like that you're confident and have a career. I mean, he did, too, obviously, but he wasn't a good guy."

"So how are you taking classes online if you can't use your real name?"

"It's not toward a degree," she said with a frown. "They're just technical classes to brush up on my skills. Truthfully, it hurt to pay their fees. Staying up-to-date is important in technology though. I need to know the latest versions of the design software that I use."

"That makes sense. And while I may be older than you, I have a feeling you're a hell of a lot smarter than me."

"I'm not," she assured him with a laugh. "Go ahead and help yourself."

He took the plate she handed him and began assembling several tacos for himself.

"Oh, I forgot the avocado!" she groaned. "I meant to grab one at the store the other day."

"Next time. Not that I'm assuming you'll feed me again, but if you're offering, I'll be here."

She flushed, and his heart swelled. Had her abusive ex never paid her a compliment? He'd never had someone to come home to and eat dinner with. Not that he expected her to be cooking for him all the time or something, but he appreciated it.

They each carried their plates to the table, Jackson somewhat surprised at how comfortable he felt with Taryn. It almost seemed like he'd known her for months, not a mere week. Their conversation flowed easily, and when they ate contentedly beside one another, it wasn't awkward.

"I hope I can finish my degree someday," she admitted. "I started it in my real name though. I can't very well go back and pick up without risking he'll find out where I am."

"Maybe he'll end up in jail anyway," Jackson said. "If your ex was that much of an asshole, no doubt he'll do something else rash."

"I don't know. Like I said, he's from the town we lived in. Everyone there thought he could do no wrong. How about you? Did you ever go to college?"

"I joined the Navy right out of high school," he admitted.

"You seemed to do pretty well for yourself," she said. "Not everyone can become a Navy SEAL. Not everyone would want to be either," she added with a laugh. "Walking around the neighborhood is about as adventurous as I get."

"Where do you walk?" he asked.

"Just around here for exercise. Or I go down to the beach on weekends. I'd love to go early in the morning, when it's calm and peaceful, but I never felt comfortable there alone. Logically, I know Austin isn't here in San Diego. I just can't shake the feeling he'll find me someday though. I feel safer there with a crowd or just sticking to the neighborhood."

Jackson frowned. Even if he did convince Taryn to eventually date him for real, she'd always be scared of her ex. And that was unacceptable to him. He knew she didn't want his help in that regard, but he also knew he'd stop at nothing to protect her.

He needed more information about her husband. Ex-husband.

"I started college," she said. "That's where we met actually. I was a sophomore, and Austin was in his fifth year there. I guess he'd failed some classes, and it took him an extra year. Then he went to the police academy. When I got pregnant, we moved back to the small town where he's from. He convinced me we'd be fine with his police career, and I still did a little design work on the side. But I never finished school. I was away from my family."

"And he hurt you," Jackson finished.

"Well, yeah. It sounds ridiculous now. I'm sure you're wondering why I didn't leave sooner. I was too terrified to do anything."

"You're safe here. Raptor is right next door. Hell, I wish I lived closer, but the second you call me, I'll be here."

"Thanks again for getting me a cell phone. I'm not sure how I can repay you—"

"You don't need to repay me," he interrupted. "It's for my peace of mind, too. And while the guys and I have PT early in the mornings, if you're ever up for a morning walk on a weekend, I'll take you."

"You'll walk on the beach with me?" she asked excitedly.

Jackson chuckled. "Of course, I will. What man would turn down walking on the beach with a beautiful woman?"

She flushed, and he decided he should put her at ease. "I don't mind avoiding the crowds either, sweetheart. It's more peaceful then. And I get that it's secluded and you don't want to be there alone. I'll pick you up early tomorrow if you want to go for a walk then."

"I'm not wearing a bikini," she said, her cheeks still pink.

"Neither will I."

She laughed, relaxing a little, and he continued. "Wear whatever you're comfortable with. If you don't want to swim, there's no need for a suit. It's actually cool this time of year for swimming. The team and I go out in wetsuits."

"I really just want to walk on the beach. Maybe next summer we can go relax on the beach and swim. I mean, not that I'm expecting you and me…." She trailed off.

"We'll take things one day at a time," he assured her. "Personally, I love that you're already thinking ahead like that. I am, too."

"I hope I'm not sending you too many mixed signals. I'm scared to ever date again, but I like you, and—" She cut herself off, looking flustered.

"I'm in no rush for anything," he said in a low voice. "And as for the summer? The guys and I love spending Saturdays on the beach when the weather is good. We can go with the whole team sometime if you want. Ghost loves to surf, and the rest of us toss a football around. We pack a ton of food. Of course, now Raptor and Ghost have women of their own, so you wouldn't have to worry about being the only woman there with my buddies and me."

"Those are their nicknames, right?"

"Yep. Every guy on the team has one. Some we got back in BUD/S and others came about a little later."

"What's yours?"

"K-Bar."

"I don't even know what that means."

"It's a knife. We train with all sorts of weapons, as I'm sure you're aware. I can hit my target dead on and earned my nickname from it."

"Well, that's kind of scary," she said with a shudder.

Jackson looked at her seriously. "Only if you're the enemy. My team and I do go in and fight the bad guys, so to speak. I'd never harm anyone unnecessarily though. I'd never hurt a woman or child. We go after HVTs—high value targets. We move in only when all the intelligence has been gathered. I don't take what I do lightly, but I'd never harm someone who didn't deserve it."

"I know. I trust you, Jackson. I may not have known you for long, but I can see how Blake is with Clarissa. He's a good guy, just like you are."

Jackson nodded then took a pull of his beer. He'd never want to scare Taryn, but she had to realize he was far more deadly than her cop ex-husband. "If you ever did want to turn in your ex to the police, I'd support you. You'd have the support of my entire team."

"They hardly know me either," she protested.

"You're with me now, and that's all that matters. Whether we date, stay friends, or any combination of the above doesn't matter. Plus, you're neighbors with Raptor and Clarissa. Even if I wasn't sitting here right now, if they heard you were in trouble, they'd be here."

"I'm not ready to report him," she said softly.

"Just know that I have your back if you ever want to. You shouldn't have to live your life afraid, under an assumed name, barely scraping by."

Jackson watched as Taryn finished her margarita. She didn't comment, and he didn't want to push her. Just last week she'd been afraid to even talk to him. Earning her complete trust would take time.

"Would you like another margarita?" he asked, changing the subject.

She shook her head no. "It was delicious, but I better stop at one tonight. Feel free to grab another beer though."

He nodded and stood, crossing over to her fridge. "I should've made something for dessert," she said, watching as he popped the cap on the longneck. "I was so nervous; I didn't think of it." He lifted his eyebrows.

"What? I wanted to make a good impression on you."

"You have made a good impression on me," he said with a chuckle. "How about we go out for ice cream?"

"Only if you let me treat."

"Not a chance," he said.

"Jackson, I have to pay for something."

"Says who?" he asked, taking the plates from her as she rose to clear the table. He put them into the sink, chuckling again as she shooed him away.

"Well, I just did, for one."

He watched in amusement as she wrapped up the rest of the food. Her dress swished around her hips as she moved, and when she stood on her tiptoes to grab a container out of the cupboard, his cock hardened at the sight of her ass.

Damn.

He needed to get a grip.

Crossing the kitchen, he pulled the balcony door shut, making sure it was locked and that the dowel he'd cut earlier fit across the lower track. It was a cheap, easy fix, and it would be impossible to slide the door open if someone jimmied the lock.

"If you're with me, I'm paying. I've got a full-time job for starters. And even if you were working in a full-time position, I wouldn't let a woman pay for me. I'd lose my man card or something."

Taryn playfully pouted at him.

"Don't give me that look," he joked.

Hell. When Taryn looked at him that way, he'd do just about whatever she wanted. Her cheeks were flushed in amusement, her eyes twinkling as they looked at him. He liked this slightly sassier side of her. She was used to being quiet and acquiescing, but he liked that she was comfortable enough with him to disagree.

"Fine, you can buy the ice cream. But only because I cooked dinner."

His lips quirked. "Fine. Are you always so stubborn?"

"More so, usually," she said with a laugh. "I used to be at any rate. You must bring out that side of me." She crossed over to him, smiling as she looked up and their gazes locked. She was such a tiny little thing in front of him, it was amusing to hear her argue with him about anything.

"I like that you're getting more comfortable with me."

Nervously, she licked her lips, and he smiled.

"I feel safe with you."

His hand reached out, lightly caressing her bare arm. She was soft and vulnerable, and he'd never felt more turned on in his entire life. Taryn was beautiful. It was her reactions around him that made his pulse pound though. He wasn't sure if she was usually shy or just uncertain how to act around a man like him.

"Can I kiss you?" he asked.

Her cheeks pinkened, but she nodded.

Gently he reached out, cupping her cheek with

one hand. She lifted a hand to his shirt, clutching the material at his side, and he could feel her tremble slightly. Jackson ducked down, brushing only the faintest hint of a kiss across her lips. He hesitated, and she moved in, kissing him back, then pulled away, her face beet red.

Jackson carefully traced his knuckles over her soft cheek. Her skin was warm, and he knew she was nervous. "We'll take things slowly," he promised her. "Just remember, you're always the one in control here. I'll never do anything you don't want."

She nodded, relaxing slightly. "I liked kissing you."

"Me too. Maybe a little too much," he joked, hoping she hadn't felt his arousal. Taryn was nervous, and he didn't need to unintentionally alarm her. He'd love to feel her body pressed against his, but now wasn't the time. Even their brief kiss had flustered her.

"How about we go get that ice cream?" he asked.

Chapter 9

Taryn walked with Jackson down the boardwalk later that evening. Maybe she should've been nervous to be practically alone with a man easily twice her size, but instead she just felt safe. Just like when they'd been alone at her townhouse.

Her eyes darted around occasionally out of habit, but even if someone did show up to harm her, she knew Jackson would never stand for it.

It was such a complete change from her old life, she couldn't quite believe it.

"It's beautiful down here," she said softly. "I love walking near the beach."

"Me too. We can still go for a walk on the beach tomorrow morning if you want." They were on the boardwalk now, and the ocean breeze lightly ruffled her dress. She shivered slightly, wishing she'd brought a sweater. She should've known that it would get cool on a fall evening here in San Diego.

Jackson's hand brushed against hers, and he gently pulled her closer to him, wrapping an arm around her shoulders. "You looked cold," he murmured.

"I am," she said. "I should've brought a sweater or something."

"We can head back to my car."

"That ice cream place was amazing," she said as they turned around. "I can't believe how many flavors they had. And that mocha fudge crunch? Oh my God."

Jackson laughed quietly. He probably didn't realize she never bought treats like that for herself. She'd been too upset to eat most of the time with Austin around, and now she simply couldn't afford to waste money on expensive ice cream. Goodness. Even the ground coffee she now had at home felt like a luxury.

"That little mom and pop ice cream shop is the best around," Jackson agreed. "I actually haven't been there in a while. I go out for a couple of beers with the guys sometimes but otherwise try to eat healthy to stay in shape."

"I'd say it's working," she said, glancing over at him.

He chuffed out a laugh. "We do PT every morning, train for hours on base, and are physically active almost 24/7 when we deploy on ops. It's grueling sometimes, but I love it."

"I'm more content to sit at my computer designing things," she admitted.

"That's a good thing. I wouldn't want you going on dangerous missions like me," he joked. "I'd worry too damn much."

"How often are you guys gone? I haven't seen Blake leave in a while. When I first moved in, it seemed like he was gone more."

"It varies a lot," Jackson admitted. "Sometimes we'll go on back-to-back missions, and sometimes we'll be home training for a while. It just depends on what's unfolding."

"That's kind of terrifying."

"We train for everything," he assured her. "I know what every man on the team is thinking when we move in on an op. I'm closer to those guys than my own family."

"Do you have any brothers or sisters?" she asked.

"I've got a younger brother. He's still in high school, so he's a hell of a lot younger than me. If I ever have kids, I'd want at least two, so they have a sibling. Hopefully a bit closer in age than we are."

"I'm an only child, and it was lonely a lot of the time."

"Do you want kids?"

"Maybe. Someday. I mean, I always did, but I told you about my pregnancy and miscarriage. It was hard. I just don't know if I'd get married again after all that."

"You never did say where you were from," he commented.

"Well, I'm from the East Coast. And I met Austin in college. We moved to a really small town after we got married." She didn't give Jackson any more details than that and wondered if he was mad. It was safer not telling him where exactly she'd run from. What if he tried to track down her ex-husband?

Jackson had seemed angry when she'd told him Austin had hit and hurt her. Would he go after the guy? Get himself in trouble and risk his Navy career? She couldn't allow him to do something like that for her. And even though she was only getting to know him, she had a feeling he'd want to hurt her ex-husband. He was the type of man who'd want to avenge her, and it wasn't worth him getting into trouble over it.

"You're not going to tell me where you lived before this, are you?" he asked quietly.

"No. At least not right now."

Jackson clenched his jaw, not saying anything for a moment. "I hate that he hurt you."

"Part of me just wants to let that part of my life go—forget it ever happened."

"I get that," he said as they walked up to his SUV. "You're not really letting it go though. You're still living in fear, running from him. Your entire life is under an assumed name."

"I know. I just feel like I can't deal with that yet."

Jackson clicked his key fob to unlock the doors, opening the passenger side one for her. He was always so attentive, the total opposite of how she'd been treated in the past. "I've got a sweatshirt in the back," he said, noticing she shivered again.

"Okay."

He closed the door and went around to the back hatch to grab it before climbing in beside her. "Here you go, sweetheart."

She gratefully put it on, inhaling the clean scent of it. "This smells like you," she said shyly. "Soap and…pine, I think."

"You smell like roses," he said with a grin.

"It's my lotion. I love floral scents, but roses have always been my favorite."

He started the engine, seeming to tuck away her comment for later use. "Huh. I kind of like you in my clothes," he said, his eyes sparking with interest as he looked over at her.

"Be careful what you say. Maybe I'll decide to keep it," she joked.

He smirked but didn't disagree.

"So where's your apartment anyway?" she asked as Jackson began to drive. "Are you near base?"

"Pretty close. Ghost has a place near me. We're not far from the beach, which is awesome. It's about twenty minutes from your townhouse. That's why I'm glad Raptor's right next door to you—not that I expect you to have any trouble," he assured her. "But I couldn't get over there as fast as I'd like in an emergency."

She swallowed, knowing he was right. She was safer with the cell phone he'd bought for her. If she continued to be careful, she wouldn't need to worry as much. She could use the phone if something ever happened.

She knew in her gut though that Austin would stop at nothing to find her. Would she ever truly feel safe without him locked up?

They drove back to her neighborhood in comfortable silence. She was tired, she realized. She hadn't had a busy day like this in so long, and the reality was, they'd done next to nothing. She hadn't been eating well, hadn't been sleeping well, and now with Jackson here, she felt as if she could fully relax.

"You look tired," he murmured.

"Yeah. Sorry. It's been a long few weeks I guess."

He gripped the steering wheel tightly as he pulled off the freeway when they reached her exit. "And you haven't been eating enough. I want you to promise me that you'll reorder some food when the groceries I got start to get low."

"You bought me more than enough."

Jackson shook his head. "They won't last forever. I know you're working hard, but I think you should save that money. I'm serious. I saved my credit card info to the grocery store's website. You can reorder when you need it."

"We'll see."

He chuckled, and she had a feeling this was an argument that she wouldn't win. If he noticed she hadn't reordered the groceries, he'd probably just do it himself. Or ask Clarissa and Blake to drop off some things for her. Sure, it was a bit bossy, but she couldn't argue that she needed to eat.

Jackson liked to take control of the situation, but unlike her ex-husband, he wanted to solve her problems. Fix things. It was quite a shock having someone in her court for a change. Taryn was so used to doing everything on her own, she almost didn't know what to make of it.

"I got a few emails yesterday about new design work."

"Really? That's awesome. New clients or new projects?"

"Both. One is a baker who needs a website for her business. The other just needed another logo designed. Hopefully the website will be something I can maintain. If I build up enough clients like that, I'll have steady work in addition to any new projects I take on."

"How do they find you?"

"I've got a website. Don't worry, it's totally different than what I used to work under. It sucked leaving my old design work and clients behind. Since

I work remotely, I could've kept them, but I basically had to cut all ties with my old life."

"That sucks, Taryn."

"It does. But now you see how I ended up struggling to get by. I'd been working my way through college and kept up with the clients I had even when Austin and I moved. I could've continued from here, but it just wasn't safe. I just put up the new website a week ago, and I'm on some of those freelance type of websites."

"And the new clients are okay not reporting the work you're doing to the IRS? I'm not sure how that all works, but you said the payments were under the table, so to speak."

"Well, yeah. I just invoice them when the work is done. I ask them to pay me over an app."

"That's tracked though, right? Through the banks or something?"

"It is, but I opened an online bank account under my new name. I transfer the funds there."

Taryn heard Jackson mutter under his breath. "I don't want you to get into trouble, Taryn. Technically, that's illegal. Opening fake bank accounts and things like that could catch up to you eventually. You don't want them to freeze your money."

"Shit, you're right." She saw Jackson's lips quirk in amusement. "What? I can't swear?"

"I don't care if you swear, sweetheart. Hell, I'm around a bunch of Navy guys all day. That was pretty mild in comparison."

"Maybe I should keep some extra cash on hand. I had to do that before in order to leave Austin. But like I told you, I ran. Unless I turn him in and deal with the police and possibly the courts—I don't know. I just don't think I can handle that. Until I can be sure he won't come after me, I have to use an alias. And that means I can't use my real name."

"We'd all be here for you—me, my buddies, their women."

"I know. It's not right to drag other people into my problems though."

"We can handle it," he assured her. "Plus, there's safety in numbers. You may not want to tell the others about your ex-husband, but wouldn't you feel better having six Navy SEALs at your back instead of just me?"

"You're impossible to argue with," she joked.

"Because I'm right."

"Maybe," she said with a sigh. "I'll think about it. This is the first week in a long time I haven't been absolutely terrified. I know it's because of you, Jackson. I'd be crazy to deny it. I've been so scared for the past couple of months, I'm not ready to open up and tell everyone my story yet."

He reached across the seat and lightly clasped her hand, his thumb running over her skin as he drove. "I don't like that you've been scared, but I swear I'll do whatever it takes to help you. To protect you."

"I know you will."

They pulled into her neighborhood, and she was surprised to see Blake and Clarissa pulling into their driveway. The fact that that shocked her was silly. Just because she usually stayed home Friday and Saturday nights didn't mean other people were hiding. And who was she kidding? She was at home every night. Every day. It was a lonely existence.

Once upon a time she'd had friends and a life. She'd go places without constantly looking over her shoulder.

Did she want to hide here forever?

Part of her longed to call her parents tomorrow and tell them where she was and that she was safe. What would Austin have told them? She'd fled so quickly, she hadn't thought much about anything but surviving. She'd slowly lost touch with most friends over the past year, and her parents had assumed she was a happy new bride.

Were they worried they hadn't heard from her in months? Angry?

Had Austin spun some story about why she didn't contact them?

Taryn had been so busy just trying to survive, she hadn't had time to worry about them. The more settled she became out here though, the more her past would catch up to her. She couldn't ignore her old life forever. But what if reaching out to them somehow led her ex-husband here?

She didn't trust him.

And despite Jackson's assurances that he'd protect her, she knew if Austin wanted to find her, he'd stop at nothing to do so.

Chapter 10

Jackson took a swig of his beer later that week, glancing around at his teammates as they sat at their favorite bar, Salty Sunset. He'd convinced Taryn to come along for a night out, and he was happy that she'd seemed to be enjoying herself for the most part. He knew she didn't go out much, but she was comfortable with the other women who were there, especially Clarissa. She wasn't scared of his friends.

Now that the size of the crowd in the restaurant was growing, however, she was much more wary than when they'd had the place to themselves. He absolutely hated the way she looked nervously at every man who walked by—like she was frightened they were someone who could harm her. Like her ex would suddenly show up here, clear across the country, and hurt her.

Raptor had noticed earlier, and the two of them had kept an eye out to make sure no one inadvertently jostled her or otherwise got into her space.

Jackson was worried though. He knew Taryn preferred the comfort and safety of her townhouse. He wanted her to be able to relax and enjoy life, not constantly live in fear. It sounded like she'd had friends, been in college, and otherwise had a relatively normal life before she met Austin. He'd love for her to have that again.

"Yo, K-Bar," Ethan said, grabbing the barstool beside him and sinking down onto it.

Taryn had gone to the ladies' room with Clarissa, Hailey, and Troy's date. He'd seen Blake murmur something to Clarissa, and he assumed his buddy was telling her to watch out for Taryn.

"No woman tonight?" Jackson asked with a smirk.

Ethan shrugged. "Nah. I went out with that one chick a few times, but it fizzled out pretty fast."

"There are lots of women here," he commented.

"I noticed. I also noticed you only have eyes for Taryn," Ethan said with a chuckle. "So what? Are you two dating now?"

"I wouldn't call it that exactly. I kissed her once, but we're taking things slowly."

Ethan's lips quirked up. "And yet here she is with you tonight. She seems a little nervous. Every time someone walks by, she's looking up like they're a potential threat. I swear she's more alert than we are."

"I know, and I don't like it," Jackson ground out. "She ran from her ex. Taryn's terrified that he'll show up someday and hurt her again."

"Shit. That's fucked up. Did she go to the police?"

"No. I'm trying to convince her that she needs to report him. Apparently, this guy is a cop though, and she doesn't think anyone will believe her."

"Where does he live?"

Jackson frowned. "She won't say. I know she came from somewhere on the east coast and that she moved to a small town. She's afraid I'll go after him or something."

"Damn straight," Ethan said. "None of us will put up with that kind of shit. And if he's a cop, he needs to lose his badge. What if he tries something like that on another woman? He's probably all sorts of crooked."

"No doubt. Hopefully I can persuade her to turn him in. It's going to take time though. She's scared, and right now, I just want her to feel safe."

"Here come our ladies!" Troy whooped, watching as their women walked back over. He jumped up to go get his date as the other men ribbed him. Troy ignored his friends and wrapped his arms around her, kissing her hard in front of everyone. His date didn't seem to mind though, and Jackson shook his head at the scene they were making.

Taryn was somewhat shy and sweet. She'd never like a public display of affection like that.

Grayson wrapped his arm around Hailey as she sat down beside him. "Well, that was quite a show," she said.

"I don't think his date minded," Grayson joked.

"Yeah, they're in their own little world," she agreed.

"How's the new job going?" Logan asked, taking a pull of his beer. "I assume things have mostly settled down now."

"It's good," Hailey assured him. "We had extra security there a couple of weeks, but now it's business as usual."

"And it better stay that way," Grayson muttered.

When Hailey had transferred to a DOD position in San Diego, someone from her old office back in Afghanistan had targeted her. After surviving the bombing in Bagram, she'd been kidnapped right here in San Diego from her office parking lot. The entire team had been looking for her, and they'd followed along on details of her new assignment once things had settled down. All the guys on the team felt protective toward her now, Jackson included.

"I heard that asshole got ten years," Logan said, referring to her kidnapper.

"That's not nearly long enough," Grayson said. "They should've locked that bastard up for life."

"He won't be allowed anywhere near a Navy base or Federal building after his actions," Jackson assured him. "And I'm glad he'll be serving time for that stunt he pulled."

His gaze flicked over to Taryn, where she stood talking with Clarissa, Troy, and his date. She brushed her dark hair back from her face, and he was happy to see her smiling. For the moment at least, she appeared relaxed. The navy-blue sweater she had on set off her fair skin, and it dipped slightly on one side, revealing a creamy shoulder.

Taryn was sexy and beautiful, and even though they'd only kissed that one time, he'd love the opportunity to pull her close one day and kiss her thoroughly. To press her body against his as he held her.

Who knew if she'd ever be comfortable enough with him to let Jackson take her to bed, but for the moment, he appreciated every chance he had to simply touch her.

Feeling his gaze on her, she glanced over and smiled. A flush spread across her cheeks, and he grinned.

Damn.

Just a look from him seemed to spark her interest. He'd love to know how she'd react if he ever got the chance to slowly undress her and kiss her everywhere. Jackson knew she hadn't been treated right by her ex-husband, and he'd love the opportunity to show her how a relationship should be.

"I never would've thought I'd be in as much danger here as in Afghanistan," Hailey said, causing Jackson's gaze to sweep back to her. "And I can't believe Kim's been missing for over a month. It's like a nightmare that just won't end."

"Not missing. Kidnapped," Ethan ground out.

Hailey let out a shaky breath. "I know, I just—I can't think of it that way. It kills me to know someone might be hurting her, and she's just over there, helpless…." Her voice trailed off, and Grayson shot Ethan an angry look as he tried to comfort his girlfriend.

Ethan drummed his fingers on the bar, agitated. "It's taking too fucking long to confirm the intel," he said in a low voice. "We should be moving in and looking for those women."

"The insurgents are tricky bastards," Jackson said. "Don't forget it took us two trips to nab Sayed," he said in a low voice, referencing the leader they'd gone after. "We could charge in now, guns blazing, and end up with the two women being killed. We need solid intel to move forward on this mission."

A loud argument drew their attention, and their

group looked over and saw two men pushing and shoving each other. They started to throw punches as they yelled, and Troy stepped in front of the women he was with, blocking them from any harm. Jackson rose and rushed over to Taryn, Ethan and Grayson hurrying to pull the angry men off one another.

Taryn was white as a ghost and trembling when Jackson reached her. "Are you all right?"

"Yeah. Wow. Those two guys are scary."

They were still screaming at one another, Jackson's teammates holding them back. He saw two bouncers moving through the crowd that had gathered, and he directed Taryn away from the mayhem.

"Are you okay?" Hailey asked. "Your hands are shaking."

"Yeah. I'm fine. That just scared me."

She shakily sat down on a bar stool, and Jackson frowned. Although the sudden argument and fight had been surprising, Taryn was the only one who seemed genuinely fearful about what had happened. He could see her trembling, and anger rose within him.

Her ex-husband was the reason she was afraid of loud, angry men. He'd hurt her, and she reacted without thought, assuming other men would, too.

"Would you rather that we leave?" he asked, placing a large hand on her bare shoulder. Her skin was supple and warm, and the soft sweater that she wore clung to her, highlighting her gorgeous breasts. At the moment, he was more worried about her mental state than how attracted he was to her though. Those guys had scared her, and his first instinct was to take Taryn somewhere she felt safe.

"Well, yes, but I know you want to visit with your

friends."

Jackson grumbled to himself. "I see those guys every day. It's you that I'm worried about. Let's head out, sweetheart. We'll go for a walk or just head home."

He glanced over at Raptor, who'd also noticed Taryn's reaction. "I'll get your tab," Blake said.

Jackson nodded. "Thanks. I owe you one."

He helped Taryn off the barstool, eager to get her out of there. He knew Raptor would settle up with the bartender, and Jackson would buy his SEAL team leader a couple of beers another time. Right now, his priority was Taryn.

Sirens sounded outside, and she stiffened. He leaned over, his lips at her ear. Her rose scent filled his nostrils, but he kept his gaze on the crowd rather than letting his eyes roam over her. "It's all right, sweetheart. None of them are your ex-husband."

"They make me nervous," she said, her voice wobbling.

Jackson could see that she was trying to hold herself together, and his chest clenched. Although he'd figured the men fighting had scared her, he hadn't considered they'd be walking out the front door right by the police as they left. She was terrified, and he hated that she felt like she couldn't trust any police officers just because of her ex-husband.

"I know they do, but I'm right here. Nothing can happen to you."

He eased his arm around her shoulders, pulling her close. Grayson frowned as he walked back over, also noticing her fear. Ethan was still standing near the men who'd been fighting, but now that the bouncers had subdued them, he was talking with Troy and his

126

date. A bouncer began yelling at the crowd to clear a path as the manager came over.

"Let's get out of here," Jackson said.

Taryn nodded but didn't move, her eyes wide.

"You're safe with me, Taryn. Let me take you home."

"Okay." Finally, she began moving toward the door, and Jackson kept her tucked protectively against his side. Police cars were pulling up in front of Salty Sunset, and he could see several officers climbing out. "It's not Austin," she said softly.

"Negative. None of them are. But I don't like seeing how scared you are, sweetheart. We'll go straight to my car and head out."

"Okay," she said again.

Jackson nodded at the police officers coming inside but directed Taryn down the block to his SUV. He knew she didn't want to tell him any details about where she was from or give him Austin's full name, but after her reaction tonight? After she'd froze in the middle of a crowded bar because she was too frightened to move?

He couldn't just let that asshole get away with terrifying her. With Taryn looking over her shoulder in fear for the rest of her life.

Jackson wanted Taryn to feel safe, and he'd do whatever was necessary for that to happen. He was going to track that bastard down and turn him in, then tell him in no uncertain terms that if he came near her ever again, Jackson would end him.

***

"Hell, sweetheart," Jackson said several minutes

later as he helped Taryn into his SUV. "I don't like seeing you so scared."

"I'm fine," she assured him. "I know I freaked out for a minute, but I'm okay. It just brought back some bad memories. Are your friends mad that we rushed out like that?"

"Mad? Of course not. They knew you were scared."

He shut the door and walked around the front of his SUV, climbing into the driver's seat. His heart caught as Taryn looked over at him. With her dark hair and the navy sweater setting off her fair skin, she looked so damn innocent it almost hurt. The fact that she'd been scared about what happened because of what she'd previously lived through made his gut churn. No woman should have to worry a man would hit her.

He hated that she lived with that fear.

"They just want to make sure you're okay. We all do." Jackson glanced down at his cell phone as it buzzed, seeing the text from Raptor.

You good?

He thumbed a quick response.

We're in my SUV. Everything's fine.

"That was one of them, wasn't it?" Taryn asked in surprise as he started the engine.

"Yep. That was Raptor."

"Wow. It's kind of amazing how you all watch out for each other."

"They're like my brothers. My family. That's why I was telling you we'd all have your back if you wanted to turn in your ex-husband. He had no right to hit you. To hurt you."

"Jackson," she pleaded. "We've been over this. I

don't want to turn him in. I know you're this invincible Navy SEAL who no one would ever bother, so you probably can't totally understand this, but he scares me. He hurt me. I'm terrified of Austin ever finding me again. It's not so easy to just bring all those memories back up by going to the police and reporting him. I'd have to relive everything."

Jackson reached over and took her hand. "You're the strongest person I know."

"I'm not strong," she protested.

"You are because you survived. It took guts to divorce him and leave, and you did it. Many women don't. And then to pack a suitcase and move clear across the country when he came after you? Not everyone could do that. I just don't like seeing you scared, sweetheart. I rushed you out of there because you were so pale, I was worried you'd pass out or something. I want you to feel safe."

"I thought they were going to hit me. I know it doesn't make sense, but I heard those angry men yelling and—" She shuddered, cutting herself off.

"Troy was right there. He'd never let some asshole touch you. Neither would I, for that matter."

She let out a shaky breath, and Jackson let go of her hand to shift out of park. He pulled away from the curb, wishing he knew a way to help Taryn. "I know you don't want to turn him in, but I could handle things. Tell me his last name, and I'll find him. I'll make sure that asshole ends up behind bars and that he never touches you again."

"I can't let you get involved like that," she said softly. "What if you got arrested and ruined your career?"

"The hell with my career. Your safety is the only

thing I'm worried about. You don't have to be involved aside from giving me his name," he assured her. "I'm sure he's done plenty of other things wrong during his time as a cop. If he's locked up, you won't need to worry and be looking over your shoulder all the time. Just tell me his last name and the town you were living in, and I'll take care of it."

"I can't tell you," she whispered.

Jackson huffed out a breath. "Why not? He shouldn't get away with this."

"He already has gotten away with it. He's living his life like nothing is wrong, and I've got nothing."

"Then let me fight for you," Jackson said, clenching his fist. "I'll help you, but you have to let me in. You have to trust me enough to be here for you."

She looked out the window as Jackson glanced over, avoiding his gaze. "Hell, Taryn, I just want to take care of you."

"I know," she said, her voice sad. "I just can't risk it right now. I'm sorry."

Chapter 11

Taryn woke up with a pounding headache the next morning. She'd tossed and turned all night, upset over arguing with Jackson. He'd walked her to her front door after they'd gotten home but hadn't come inside. Taryn knew he'd wanted to talk things over, but she'd just needed to be alone.

He'd looked almost hurt that she hadn't given him Austin's last name. Jackson had been nothing but sweet and attentive to her the past couple of weeks, but his wanting to avenge her wouldn't solve anything. He could get in trouble for threatening a police officer, and it wasn't worth Jackson risking his career over it.

When she was ready—if she was ever ready—she could turn Austin in herself.

It was easier said than done, but she did have the option. She could file a police report stating that he hurt and threatened her. And if she ever went to the police, it would be her choice. It wouldn't be Jackson deciding when things needed to be taken care of; it would fall on her shoulders.

She'd left her ex determined to live her own life, and even if Jackson did have her best interests at heart, she couldn't let him decide something like this that would impact her entire life. She'd have to relive all of it, and she was finally feeling a bit more settled here. She knew a few people. She'd found a new client. She'd saved a very small amount.

She couldn't confront her past until she felt stronger. Less raw over everything that had happened to her over the past year. And who knew if that would ever happen.

Tears smarted her eyes as she recalled Jackson's words on her front porch.

"Give me a chance to protect you, sweetheart—to love you."

She'd been shocked. Was he already falling in love with her? They'd briefly kissed one time, but otherwise hadn't shared much physical intimacy. Still, she felt safer with him than anyone. She was attracted to him. They'd had dinner together several times, and he'd been coming by when he could after work. She knew all his friends. She'd even told him about her potential new design work and shown him some of the websites she'd created. Jackson had been nothing but supportive as they'd gotten to know one another, and he'd held her when she cried, but she'd refused to tell him any more details about her past.

And even last night, when she'd been upset, she'd still felt a pull toward him as they stood on her porch. He was muscular and handsome, but it was the look in his eyes that called out to her soul. It was heated and possessive, but she knew he'd always be gentle with her. If she gave her heart to him, she knew he'd never hurt her.

But she hadn't let him come in.

They'd said goodnight, Jackson trying not to appear too irritated that she was keeping her past to herself, and she'd gone into her house alone, almost in tears.

Sighing, she climbed out of her bed. She couldn't wallow around in misery all morning. She had some new design work to do, and she knew at some point she and Jackson would talk things over. It wasn't that they'd truly argued. He'd just been upset she wouldn't let him further into her life.

Taryn pulled a delicate robe on over her camisole and sleep shorts and walked downstairs to her kitchen. She'd been thrilled to find a few summer items on clearance when she'd stopped by a local big box store. Her one suitcase of clothes had been enough in the beginning, but adding a couple of more items to her wardrobe meant she didn't need to do laundry as frequently. And it wasn't like she'd gone out and splurged on designer fashion.

She couldn't help but wonder what Jackson would think if he ever saw her in any of it. It wasn't meant to be sexy lingerie, but it was feminine and pretty. Even if it had been inexpensive, she felt comfortable and attractive in it.

Not that she'd be inviting him over to spend the night any time soon.

Her cell phone buzzed as she made a pot of coffee, and she frowned. Jackson had called her on it a few times, but she generally didn't use it all that much. She knew he'd added more minutes to her plan, because they had talked on a couple of occasions. He wasn't much for long phone calls though, and she preferred seeing him in person anyway. The phone was fine for a question or making plans, but they didn't sit around talking for hours every night.

Besides, he was likely on base right now. The men had PT every morning and then spent their days in briefings, drilling, and who knew what else.

She couldn't imagine anyone else needing to reach her though.

"Hey, it's me," Jackson said as she answered.

"Hi. Is everything okay?"

"It is, but I have to head out."

"Head…out?"

"We're being sent out on a mission," he said hurriedly. "I never know how much notice I'll get ahead of time, but we're going wheels up in a few hours."

"Oh."

"I'm sorry I won't get to see you before we leave. I have to prepare with the team right now. I feel awful about how we left things last night. I don't want you upset with me."

"It's all right," she said quietly.

"It's not, and it kills me that I can't come over right now. Taryn, I feel terrible. I know I pushed you for information, but that's only because I want to make sure you're safe. Because I care about you."

"I know." She sniffled as tears smarted her eyes, and she heard his moan of frustration on the other end of the phone.

"Damn it. I wish I had time to come by and talk to you in person. It kills me that you're upset."

"I'm not upset," she assured him. "I'm just sad that you're leaving, and I didn't sleep well—"

"Because you were upset with me," he finished. "I would've come inside to talk last night, but you asked me to leave, and I felt like I had to respect your wishes."

"I know. I just feel silly about arguing with you now. How long will you be gone?"

"I'm not sure. I can't tell you where I'm going or when I'll be back, but I would never just leave without letting you know."

"I understand. This is your job. I've known all along you'd have to go at some point." A tear rolled down her cheek anyway, and she knew she was being foolish. This had nothing to do with her disagreement with Jackson last night. This was his career. He'd warned her that he got called out without notice sometimes. Goodness. She'd asked him herself about it since Blake had been home more than usual.

She didn't know what exactly they did before leaving, but she assumed it involved packing clothes, gear, weapons, and whatever the heck else they used.

"I just found out from my commander," he said gruffly. "I was hoping to come by and see you tonight. I'm sorry we argued yesterday."

She sniffled again slightly, hoping he didn't hear it.

"Hell. Are you crying?" he asked, his voice anguished.

"No. I'm fine."

"Taryn."

"I understand that you have to go. It's your job. Just please be careful, okay?"

"I will. And you have to promise me that you'll be careful, too. Call Clarissa if you notice anything unusual. She'll be able to get in touch with my commander or some of the other guys on base."

"I'll be okay," she assured him.

"Shit. I have to go. I hate this, but I'll talk to you as soon as I get back, sweetheart."

A beat passed, and she wondered what on earth she should say. There wasn't time for anything now. He was in a hurry to pack and leave, and she was still feeling unsettled about last night, only to find out he wouldn't even be here for a while.

"Okay. Please be safe, Jackson."

"I will. Bye, sweetheart."

She opened her mouth, but he'd already disconnected the call. "Shit," she whispered, a few more tears slipping down her cheeks. Why hadn't she just smoothed things over with him last night? She could've invited him in, talked things over, and gotten a restful sleep. Now she was tired, upset, and worried about him.

Blowing out a sigh, she sank down at her kitchen table. She was falling for Jackson, she realized. Hard. She could claim she didn't date all that she wanted, but the reality was, they were together. He came over after work, called her to see how she was, and told her he'd be gone. Hopefully she hadn't screwed up everything by refusing to let him into her heart.

***

Three days later, Taryn sat at her laptop working. It was lonely as hell going back to her old routine, and she'd only known Jackson a few short weeks. She missed seeing him though. She missed talking to him in the evenings when he swung by after work. She missed the deep sound of his voice and even the clean, pine scent of his soap. She'd felt safe every time he'd held her, and even though they hadn't done more than kiss, she longed for him to come back and assure her everything between them would be okay.

Could she be brave enough for a real relationship, though?

She'd find out when he got home. Whenever that was.

After scanning over an email from a potential client, she sent them a few additional design samples. She had some of her newer work up on her own website, but they'd been interested in seeing more. Some designers had large portfolios. She hadn't put everything online for fear that Austin would somehow track her down. She didn't think he'd paid too much attention to her college classes and work as a graphic designer, but she couldn't be too careful.

Taryn was surprised to receive an email from them right away.

Those are fantastic! We'd be interested in a website for our new business. Can we set up a time for a phone call? What time zone are you in?

Typing a quick response, she sent the email. It was certainly easier to do things over the phone sometimes. They could discuss ideas and the project timeline before they settled on a contract.

She jumped as her phone buzzed, and then she nearly laughed for being so silly. The potential new client didn't have her phone number. It was only Clarissa sending her a text. And even if someone did call her one day for business-related purposes, that didn't mean it was her crazy ex-husband.

Hi! Are you doing okay?

Taryn quickly thumbed a response back.

I miss him.

She could almost see Clarissa smiling before her phone buzzed again.

I know. Want to come over for lunch?

Taryn quickly texted her back to coordinate. Lunch with a friend was just what she needed. If she admitted it to herself, she was feeling a bit down in the dumps. She missed Jackson and was feeling unsettled with how they'd left things. Plus, she'd never dealt with anything like this before. She didn't know where he was, if he was okay, or even when he'd be home.

And who was she kidding?

If something happened to him, she'd have to rely on Clarissa or Hailey to tell her. She and Jackson weren't married. They didn't live together. The U.S. Navy didn't even know she existed. Jackson had said Clarissa knew the commander and some other guys from base. Maybe she'd have an update.

Although they weren't super close yet, she'd enjoyed getting to know her neighbor. It would be nice to have someone to talk with even if just for a little while.

Taryn made plans for a call with her potential new client later that week and finished up some other design changes she'd been working on. At noon, she grabbed the tequila and triple sec Jackson had brought that one night and headed over to Clarissa's. They weren't normally "day drinkers" but had agreed they'd each have a margarita and relax over lunch. They couldn't do dinner since Clarissa had a lecture that evening, but a long lunch break would do a world of good. Clarissa had ordered some food from a local café that delivered, and Taryn was more than ready to hang out for a little while and get her mind off Jackson.

Clarissa smiled as she opened the door. "Hi! Thanks for bringing those. I've got plenty of limes and sugar to make margaritas. We really should get together one night for a girls' night. The guys are gone. Maybe on Friday or Saturday if they're not home yet? I can see if Hailey wants to come, too."

"Yeah, that'd be fun," Taryn agreed. "I have to admit I've been feeling a little lonely. It's weird because I'm so used to being alone," she said as she came inside. "Jackson started dropping by after work though."

"I noticed," Clarissa said with a smile.

Taryn flushed, not knowing quite why she felt embarrassed by his attention. Jackson liked her. She'd been nervous to pursue anything, but goodness. Now that he was gone, she missed him more than ever. She couldn't let her fears rule her life.

"He's sweet," Clarissa said. "I know you just started dating or whatnot, but I can tell he cares about you."

"We got into an argument before he left," Taryn said with a frown as she followed Clarissa into the kitchen.

"Well, it happens. I can't pretend Blake and I get along one hundred percent of the time. He works long hours, and I'm mostly busy in the evenings now. The weekends are when we see each other more even though we live in the same house. We'll go hiking or camping and just get away from our day-to-day life and reconnect."

"How's the wedding planning coming?"

"It's not," she said with a laugh. "I'm pretty laid back. I bought all those bridal magazines but just kind of flipped through them. I'll go dress shopping of course, but a casual beach wedding is fine with me."

"I was married," Taryn admitted.

Clarissa nearly dropped the margarita glass she was getting out of the cupboard. "You were? Wow. I had no idea. You seem so young."

"Yeah, I am. I was. We're divorced, but it didn't end well."

"Wait—that's the guy Blake said was threatening you?"

"He told you?" Taryn asked, her mouth dropping open.

Clarissa turned to fully face her. "He did. It wasn't to gossip or make you feel awkward or anything. Jackson was worried about you. I'm sure it's unlikely your ex-husband would find you here—it sounds like you moved far away, right?"

"I did. I'm sorry for not saying anything."

"You don't owe me an explanation," Clarissa assured her. "We barely just started hanging out. I don't expect to know your entire life story. I haven't even really told you about how Blake and I met. But my point was, Jackson was worried. The guys just wanted me to know so I could help look out for anything suspicious."

"I understand. It makes sense. It's just embarrassing to have everyone know about what I dealt with."

"Taryn, I was kidnapped. I hired a guide so I could do research in the Colombian rainforests and assumed I could handle myself. They killed him and kidnapped me. No one even knew I was missing.

Blake and his team were there for another reason, and he literally just stumbled upon me. If they didn't find me?" She closed her eyes tightly.

"I'm sorry," Taryn said quietly. "I can't imagine."

"We all go through crazy stuff," Clarissa said. "Some of it is obviously worse than others. But Jackson and Blake? Those guys see it all. We don't even know about their missions and what they deal with. I saw when they rescued me, but wow. The rest of it, I'll never know."

Taryn let out a breath. "I just feel silly for falling for a guy that was abusive."

"You didn't know, right? I'm sure he didn't act like that all along. That's how people like that work. They charm you into liking them and then reveal their true selves."

"Well, no, he wasn't always abusive," Taryn said, watching as Clarissa grabbed some limes from the fridge and began juicing them. "He was nice at first—maybe a little bossy, but not necessarily in a bad way."

"And he has no idea you're here now?"

"No. I left everything behind—my apartment, my old clients, my entire life. I changed my name."

"That was smart," Clarissa said. "Do you have credit cards or anything he can use to track you?"

"I have one for emergencies that's still in my old name, but I don't use it. We were divorced, but he was still stalking and threatening me. Finally, I did the only thing that I could—I ran."

"That was so brave of you."

"It wasn't," Taryn said. "I could've turned him in. That's what Jackson and I argued about. He wanted me to give him Austin's last name and the town where we lived."

"And you wouldn't?"

"I'd have to relive everything," Taryn said. "I'd have to file a report with the police, tell them everything that happened. And my ex is a cop. He knows those guys."

"Can you file a police report here?"

"I…don't know. I'm not sure how it works, to be honest. Jackson said he'd go with me." She let out a shaky breath. "I just feel terrible that we argued right before they left. Jackson wanted to come inside and talk more, but I asked him to leave."

"It was after the night at the bar, right? When those guys there got in a fight?"

Taryn nodded.

"You looked terrified," Clarissa said. "I know Jackson just wants to protect you. It's hard for those guys to just sit back and do nothing."

"I get it, but I also wanted him to understand it had to be my decision. I'm scared to death of Austin. It's not so easy just to tell the police my story."

The doorbell rang, and Clarissa glanced over. "That's the food. I'll be right back."

Taryn finished making the margaritas while her friend went to the front door. She listened to her talking to the driver, and then the door shut, and Clarissa was heading back upstairs.

"I'll text Hailey and see if she's up for a girls' night this weekend," Clarissa said as she set the bags down on the kitchen table. Taryn brought the margaritas over.

"Sorry again we couldn't do dinner," Clarissa said.

"It's no problem. My schedule is totally flexible. I've got deadlines for my client work, but I basically just work when I want to."

"And the class?"

"I just finished the nine-week course I was taking. It wasn't the same as a regular semester-long class. I'm not sure I'll do any more since they're expensive. This was online through my old college. I had a partial credit to use, so I didn't have to pay for it."

"Huh. Could your ex-husband track you that way?"

"I don't see how. He knew where I was attending school. That's where he came to stalk me after we got divorced. I'm guessing he figured I dropped out when I left town."

"So you have your old email address and stuff?" Clarissa asked.

"The school one, yes. I changed everything for work though. I had to create a new website for my graphic design business, including a new email and name. I started from scratch. I'm slowly building up more clients again, so I hope to have a steadier stream of income."

"That's amazing you were able to accomplish all that."

Taryn shrugged. "I was doing it before. I basically just started my business over. It sucks, but I did what I had to."

"It is an accomplishment though," Clarissa insisted. "You're young. You should be proud of everything you've done for yourself."

Taryn felt herself blushing. She admired and respected Clarissa, and it meant a lot to hear her compliment. Jackson seemed impressed with what she'd managed as well. It was nothing compared to his accomplishments in the military, but she did appreciate their support.

The two women dug into their food, sipping on their margaritas and talking.

"I guess you haven't heard anything from Blake?" Taryn asked.

"No. We usually wouldn't unless there was an emergency—like an injury or something. Then their commander would let me know. If they're gone a really long time, I can try to get in touch with one of the other SEALs from base. There are a couple of teams. I don't really know them very well though, so I don't talk to them on a regular basis or anything."

"I didn't think it would be this hard," Taryn admitted. "I knew what Jackson did and that he could deploy at any time, but living it is different."

"And they're not usually gone for long missions," Clarissa said. "Can you imagine having your boyfriend or girlfriend deploy for an entire year? So many military families deal with worse, so I feel like I can't complain."

"You're right. I'm just feeling sorry for myself. I didn't get to see Jackson before he left. He called me from base, and I started crying. We hadn't left things on a good note the night before."

"I'm sorry," Clarissa said. "That's hard. But he called you because he cares about you. It would've been worse to not even hear from him at all."

"Absolutely. I would've been devastated."

"I would've told you they left," Clarissa assured her.

"I know, but it would've hurt for Jackson not to even say goodbye."

"You have to be strong, but I know you already are. They'll be back before we know it, you guys will kiss and make up, and then we'll all live happily ever after."

"Until they leave again," Taryn said dryly.

Clarissa took a sip of her margarita, her eyes twinkling. "Yes, but the reunions when they return are always pretty fun."

Taryn giggled, surprising herself. She'd been terrified to ever be with a man again, but what would it be like if she ever spent the night with Jackson? To have him touch and hold her. To make love. She knew he'd take things as slowly as she needed, but wow. She hadn't thought she'd ever get there just a few short weeks ago. Missing him this much made her realize she wanted him in her life.

Hopefully it wasn't too late to tell him how she really felt.

Chapter 12

Jackson grumbled as the team convened in the small, cramped hut that afternoon. They'd been gone for a week and still hadn't found the terror cell leader they were tracking across Algeria. Moving through the confined space, he looked down at the map of the region spread out across the dusty table.

"The latest intelligence from our source indicates he's moved here," Blake said, pointing with a gloved hand to the map.

"That's less than two miles away. How solid is this source?" Troy asked, frowning. "Two days ago, they thought he'd fled to the other side of the country."

Ethan crossed his arms, glancing around at the others. "We can't very well chase him across North Africa. If the intelligence is good, let's grab this mofo and go home."

"The source is reliable, and the location was confirmed by signals intelligence of movement in the area," Blake confirmed. "Commander Hutchinson has ordered us to move in tonight."

Jackson scrubbed a hand across the stubble on his jaw as Blake gave them some additional information. He was tired and dirty after tracking this latest asshole across the desert with his teammates. Their commander had given them word a week ago that one of the most wanted terrorists in the world had been sighted here in Algeria. His team had been deployed immediately, but the mission was lasting longer than any of them wanted.

Luckily it sounded like the man hadn't escaped. Whereas on their last op to Afghanistan, they'd lost Abdul Sayed only to nab him a few weeks later, this guy was still here. Within reach. The team would move in and eliminate one more evil jihadist from the world.

In the back of his mind, Jackson was also worried about Taryn. His gut churned at the tears he'd heard in her voice when he'd called to say he was leaving. He wished like hell he hadn't pushed her for information on the night before their op. He'd always told himself he'd tread carefully with her. Although she hadn't been frightened by him, clearly, she'd been upset. And that made him want to rip his own heart right out.

He hadn't gotten to smooth things over before he'd left, and the guilt was eating at him. He'd promised he'd protect her, yet for the first op he'd been sent on after they'd met, he'd left after they'd argued. Fucking hell.

Blake caught his eye as the others talked strategy for moving in at nightfall. "You okay, K-Bar?"

"Yep."

"It sucks leaving your woman behind," Blake commented.

"She's not my woman."

His team leader chuckled. "Sure. You're just over there at her place every night for no reason."

Jackson clenched his fist. "I'm not saying I don't want her as my woman—just that she's hesitant to get into another relationship."

"Hesitant or not, I'd say you're already in one. Call it whatever you want, but when you're going over every night, spending time with her, you're dating. A couple."

"She was mad at me when we left," Jackson admitted.

"Shit happens. No relationship is perfect all the time. You can't expect it to be, either."

"I know. I just feel guilty as hell for leaving her when we hadn't gotten a chance to talk about things. And in the back of my mind, I'll always be concerned knowing her asshole of an ex is out there."

"She's smart," Blake said. "She was smart enough to divorce him and run. She'll be smart enough to take care of herself now."

"I hope you're right. It just eats at me that I'm not there to protect her."

"You have to trust that she'll do the right thing. It's hard as hell, but she's an adult. You can't be at her side twenty-four seven, even if you might want to be."

"Doesn't make it any easier though," Jackson muttered.

"Are you two finished with your chitchat?" Ethan asked, looking over at them in annoyance. "We've got things to discuss."

"Roger that, asshole," Jackson said, glaring at him.

Blake chuckled. "You fellas got a plan? Because I'm all for sneaking in tonight and kicking some terrorist ass."

***

Taryn's heart jumped as her phone buzzed on the kitchen table the next morning. Given that she'd scheduled the call herself, it was a silly reaction. She needed to discuss with her potential new client what they wanted for their new website.

She hated talking on the phone though, preferring instead to communicate via email. And although she'd known it wasn't Jackson when her phone buzzed, a tiny part of her hoped he'd been calling to say he was home and rushing over to see her. Right at the exact time of her client call. Sure.

The past week had gone by painstakingly slow, and it was harder than she'd expected not knowing when Jackson would return. Would he even want to see her right away? He'd probably be exhausted and just head home to crash. It's not like he'd been spending the night here.

And they hadn't exactly left things on great terms.

Shaking her head as she tried to clear her thoughts, she grabbed her cell phone.

"This is Taryn," she said.

Although the potential client had asked if she did video conference calls, she'd opted not to. She'd been in video chats for the class she'd just finished, but she'd kept her camera and microphone off while the instructor taught the students. She didn't feel comfortable video chatting with a stranger she didn't know or with the idea of them seeing inside her home.

And there was always the fear in the back of her mind that her ex-husband would somehow find her. She certainly didn't need someone to take a screenshot of her and share her photo all over the place. It was unlikely, no doubt, but she wasn't about to let her guard down now.

"Hi Taryn. Chris Palmer," a male voice said. "We emailed a few days ago."

Instantly the hair on the back of her neck rose. She'd never met anyone by that name, but something about the voice seemed slightly familiar.

She nervously cleared her throat. "Hi Chris. You're interested in a website design, correct? Why don't you tell me a little about your business and vision?"

"Sure thing. It's a new venture, so we're starting fresh. You said you're on the west coast, right?"

"Pacific time zone," she said automatically without revealing anything else. They'd already covered that when setting up the time for their call.

"Fantastic. It's nice to be able to work from anywhere nowadays, isn't it?"

"Um-hmm," she said. "So, tell me about what you hope to have for your website. Is this a one-time design or will you require website maintenance?"

Taryn heard a muffled voice in the background and furrowed her brows. Was this guy calling from an office? It wasn't really a conference call since only the two of them were on the line. Were his business partners listening in or something?

"Are you still there?" she asked when she didn't hear a reply. "Chris?"

She started to feel nervous for some reason. She

got the strange vibe that someone was listening in to their conversation. She hadn't told them any personal information, but something just seemed off. Usually, clients were happy to talk about their business needs. This guy hadn't even answered a single question yet.

"Listen, I apologize, but I'm going to have to reschedule. Let me shoot you an email to set up a new time. Goodbye."

The phone disconnected, and she stared at her own phone in confusion. That was the weirdest call ever. They'd picked the time and still hadn't provided any information on what they were looking for.

Shaking her head, she set her phone down and checked her email. She had other work to do aside from worrying about flaky clients. If they emailed her again, she wouldn't respond. The whole call had been weird. She couldn't quite put her finger on it, but she had a weird feeling. No matter. The woman who'd contacted her about a website for her bakery had signed a contract, and Taryn had her other projects to do. She didn't need to do business with someone who made her uncomfortable.

Tomorrow night she'd get together with Clarissa and Hailey, and hopefully sometime over the next week Jackson would be back. In the meantime, she'd focus on work, just like she'd always done. She'd keep her head down and get her things done, and life would go on, just like it always had before.

Chapter 13

Taryn stood up and stretched Friday afternoon, ready to shut down her laptop for the day and take a long walk. She had girls' night next door at seven with Clarissa and Hailey, and she wanted to get some fresh air, shower, and change before she headed over.

Jackson and his SEAL team had been gone for more than a week, and her uneasiness had grown even stronger today. She didn't know what it was, but something in the back of her mind was putting her senses on high alert.

Had Jackson been hurt?

Was he in danger?

She knew those guys dealt with dangerous situations. Clarissa had told her she'd been kidnapped by a terrorist group. No doubt Jackson dealt with the worst of humanity. Taryn knew soldiers and other military personnel were deployed to the Middle East.

Was that where Jackson was?

She didn't have a TV, but she'd searched the Internet for any news stories about U.S. military forces being injured. She knew Jackson didn't advertise to the world that he was a SEAL, but if something had gone haywire, it would be on the news. Hailey had been part of that bombing in Bagram, and Taryn knew about that.

She shuddered. What were the chances her two closest friends here had dealt with such awful situations? It made her own abusive marriage seem almost mild in comparison. Austin had been awful, but he wasn't a terrorist threatening to kill multiple Americans.

Taryn went upstairs to change into running tights and a workout camisole. She walked rather than jogged but had managed to pack some of her workout clothes when she'd fled Pennsylvania. Frowning, she realized she'd never told Jackson where she was from. She knew about his family and military career, and she'd mostly kept her life under wraps. No wonder he'd been frustrated.

Shaking her head, she quickly changed and then pulled her long dark hair back into a ponytail. She'd grab her cell phone and keys before she left. She double-checked the sliding glass door off her kitchen, despite the fact that she hadn't opened it. Would she ever stop freaking out about making sure every door and window were locked? She doubted it.

Taryn went out the front door and locked it, walking down the steps toward her driveway. She frowned as she heard a dog barking in her backyard. It was a small, fenced-in area below her deck. She never used it as it was shady and mostly just weeds, but there was a gate that allowed access.

The hair on the back of her neck stood up as she approached the gate. It was shut, which meant someone had to have opened it to let the dog inside. She didn't think there was another way for a dog to get in. The fence was solid, not rotting away or something. Briefly, she glanced over at Clarissa's house. She almost went over but decided that was silly. What exactly could her friend do?

Taryn would open the gate and let the dog out. It didn't sound aggressive or angry; it simply had barked a few times.

She reached for the handle, pulling the gate open. A small dog came running up, happily barking and wagging its tail. "Hi doggy!" she said, stepping aside and watching it run off. She thought she'd seen it on one of her walks around the neighborhood. What was it doing in her backyard though?

Turning back toward her small yard, she looked around. She didn't see any signs that someone else was there.

Why would one of her neighbors have put a dog in her backyard though?

Taryn walked into the backyard, looking around. The lawn was more weeds than grass, some of it dead from the cooler autumn nights. She really should clean the area up, but she didn't have any yard tools or even a weedwhacker. The bushes off to the side needed to be trimmed, but there were no holes or damage to the fence.

She took another step, looking around, and then froze as she saw Austin in the shadows under her deck.

He was pointing a gun at her, and she was afraid to even move a muscle. She should've run or screamed, but instead she stood motionless in place as he stalked toward her. "Not a fucking word, bitch," he said, grabbing her by the upper arm and yanking her toward him. He pulled her against his muscular body, his hand covering her mouth, the gun at her temple.

Austin moved them forward, back toward the area underneath her deck as she shook in fear.

Taryn heard a car door slam shut across the street and whimpered, and Austin hustled them into the shadows under the deck. Even though she had neighbors on both sides of her townhouse, the space under the deck was covered and secluded. It was part of the reason she never came out here.

She trembled as Austin tightened his arm, forcing her to move with him.

"Fuck! There's no door down here?" he spat out, shoving her to the ground in anger. She fell to her knees, wincing as the rocks on the ground bit into her hands. The thin running pants she had on did little to protect her either. She knew Austin had assumed she had a basement door. Didn't most houses? She had a very small basement, but most of the space at the bottom level of the townhouse was taken up by the garage. There was no access to the backyard unless you used the gate.

She scrambled away, panicked, but Austin was on her in an instant. He pushed her down into the dirt and rocks, straddling her body so she couldn't move. "Don't fucking make a sound or I'll shoot you," he said, smacking her in the temple with his gun.

Pain lanced through her, and she whimpered again in fear. She was face down on the ground, and Austin could do whatever he wanted. He grabbed her ponytail, pulling her head back and smashing it to the ground again. She cried out, and he shoved his gun into her temple again.

"You thought you could run, didn't you, Tara?" he sneered. "I scoured the Internet for months looking at graphic designer websites. You thought I wouldn't realize you'd start up a new business? You're mine, bitch, and I'm not letting you get away again."

He leaned down, his breath on her neck, and lightly kissed her skin. She shivered in disgust, hating the fear creeping down her spine. He smelled of alcohol, and she wondered if he'd spent the day drinking. "You make me crazy," he muttered, keeping the gun at her head as he shifted slightly above her. He palmed her ass, squeezing it, and she started to cry, fearful he was going to rape her right there in her backyard.

"Please let me go," she pleaded.

"Never. I'm never letting you go," he hissed, leaning down again. He nipped at her neck with his teeth, his hand trying to inch beneath her stomach. "You made a fool of me at the police department. How do you think it made me look when we got divorced so quickly? Fucking bitch!" he said, lifting his hand back up and punching her in the side.

She gasped, and he hit her again.

Before she could say anything else, he flipped her over, moving on top of her as he punched her in the face. She cried out again, squeezing her eyes shut.

"Look at me!" he hissed.

She did as he asked, tears streaming down her cheeks. Austin had a crazed look in his eyes, and one hand slid to her neck as her head throbbed in pain. "I should fucking kill you for the way you treated me," he said, lightly gripping her neck. "I don't think I can live without you though."

Another car door shutting had him looking up. "Shit. Why the fuck are all your neighbors coming home right now?" He met her fearful gaze. "Are you afraid of me, princess?" He squeezed her neck slightly harder as she tried to swallow. "You're mine. All of you."

Taryn whimpered as his fingers touched her temple, where he'd first hit her with the gun. She was shocked to see blood on them. Her head throbbed and her ribs hurt, but he hadn't hit her hard enough to draw blood, had he?

Holding the gun to her head, he squeezed her neck harder. Gasping for breath, she lifted her hands to his arm, trying to pull it off of her.

"Don't make me fucking shoot you," he growled.

He squeezed harder, and her vision began to blur. Was he going to choke her to death right here? That was her last thought before everything went black.

Chapter 14

Jackson grumbled as they strode off the plane after arriving back in California. It had been a hell of a long flight home. He was tired and exhausted, but the team had successfully taken out the terrorist cell leader in Algeria. They'd moved in that night exactly as planned, and after two different flights, were back on U.S. soil at last.

Blake glanced over at the team. "The CO said we can debrief at oh eight hundred."

"Thank fuck for small miracles," Grayson said, rolling his shoulders as he walked. "I'm going to shower after we stash this gear and get home to Hailey."

"Are you going to Taryn's?" Blake asked, raising his eyebrows.

"Affirmative. I'll shoot her a text then quick change before I head over. I know we've got meetings tomorrow, but I hope like hell we'll get a couple of days off afterward."

"You and me both," Blake quipped.

The team walked into one of the buildings on base, stashing some of their equipment and gear for subsequent missions. Jackson texted Taryn before he headed toward the showers, wanting to rid himself of the dirt and grime he'd acquired after trekking across the desert for a few days. He didn't want to show up at Taryn's house looking like he hadn't showered in a week, which unfortunately, was the truth at the moment.

"All right, sweetheart, I'll see you soon," Blake said, grinning as he stuck his phone into his locker.

Jackson raised his eyebrows. "The women had planned on drinks at our place tonight," Blake said with a chuckle. "Let's just say Clarissa was more than happy to reschedule."

"I didn't hear back from Taryn."

"She's probably just getting ready. Want me to ask Clarissa to let her know we're back?"

Jackson lifted a shoulder. "Sure. I kind of wanted to surprise her, but given the fact that we argued, it's probably better for her to know that I'm coming."

"Roger that," Blake said, grabbing his phone again.

Jackson showered and changed with record speed. He'd be back in the a.m. soon enough for briefings with their commander, but at the moment, he couldn't wait to get over to Taryn's. He was exhausted as hell, but he knew he couldn't sleep until he pulled her into his arms. He felt guilty that he'd pressured her about more information on Austin, and the moment he saw her tonight, he'd reassure her that they'd move at her pace. When she wanted to go to the police, they could. He wouldn't push her for more than she was ready for yet.

Jackson climbed into his SUV, noticing Raptor's was still in the parking lot. He chuckled to himself quietly. Yep, he was ready to see his woman. And Taryn was his. Whether they officially called themselves a couple or not, he knew that they were meant for one another. She hadn't texted him back yet, but at this point, he'd be at her place soon enough. Hopefully she'd seen his text or Clarissa had let her know he and his teammates were back.

Pulling into her neighborhood fifteen minutes later, he immediately knew something was wrong. A police car was in front of Taryn's house, and Clarissa was there, knocking on the front door. Jackson pulled to a stop and frowned as he saw a smashed cell phone in the driveway where an officer was standing.

Taryn's phone.

But where the hell was she?

Jackson jumped out of his SUV and rushed toward the house. "Where's Taryn?" he called out.

Clarissa looked back at him. "I don't know. She was supposed to come over for drinks. She didn't show up, and I thought she was just running late. Then Blake called, and I came over here since he said you couldn't reach her. I saw her smashed cell phone in the driveway and called 911."

"Good job," Jackson assured her. He knocked on the front door himself, louder than Clarissa just had. "Taryn! It's me. Jackson. We just got back. Are you in there?"

"I've been knocking for ten minutes," Clarissa said worriedly.

The police officer was radioing in to the dispatchers when Blake pulled up. He immediately jumped out of his SUV as Jackson had just done. Blake hadn't even showered or changed yet, and Jackson assumed he'd been delayed dealing with something on base. "What's wrong?" he barked out.

"Taryn is missing!" Clarissa called back.

The officer looked at him, taking in his fatigues and dirty appearance. "We're Navy SEALs," Blake said as he rushed over. "We just got back from a mission, and Jackson is Taryn's boyfriend. What happened here?"

The officer began explaining the few things they knew, and Jackson's eyes swept up and down the front of Taryn's townhouse. He'd helped Taryn secure the place himself. He knew the front door had the strong deadbolt he'd purchased and installed, so it would be hard to break in. The windows all looked shut. But was Taryn even inside?

He tried the doorknob, just in case Clarissa hadn't yet, but it was locked. Rushing back down the steps, he looked around. Her car looked fine, with the doors shut. The garage door was closed. "I'll check around back," he said.

"Ten-four," the officer said into his radio. "There's no damage aside from the smashed cell phone. The property is secure on the front. I'll look around some more."

"Do any of you have a key to her house?" he asked.

Clarissa and Blake both looked to Jackson. "No, I don't."

He kept moving past the officer and toward the fenced-in backyard. Jackson frowned as he saw that the gate wasn't fully shut. Taryn never went into her backyard and always kept the gate closed. Was someone back there?

"Raptor!" he called out.

Jackson didn't know what he'd find back there, but his senses were already on high alert. Maybe it was adrenaline left over from their mission, but he felt on edge and wanted his teammate at his side.

Blake was behind him in an instant, and the two men exchanged a glance. Blake immediately noticed the same thing he did—the gate was open. Without thought, Jackson pulled the knife he had on from the back of his waistband. If someone had hurt Taryn, they wouldn't fucking get away.

Blake moved beside him, grabbing his own knife, and then Jackson yanked on the gate, the two men bursting into the tiny backyard. There was no movement, nothing amiss, as Jackson's gaze swept the perimeter. It looked overgrown, and he silently cursed that he hadn't offered to help her clean up the space.

Blake took a step to the right, looking on the ground for any clues. A low moan caught their attention though, and both men looked toward the deck.

A woman lay battered on the ground, and then Jackson was running toward her without thought.

Taryn.

"Fucking hell. We need an ambulance!" Blake yelled. "Hurry! She's been hurt!"

Jackson heard a commotion as Clarissa, the police officer, and some of the neighbors began rushing into the backyard. Sirens sounded in the distance as more police and emergency vehicles were called. But all he could see was Taryn. She was crumpled on the ground with a black eye and dried blood at her temple, plus bruising around her throat. She moaned again, clutching onto her ribs, as Jackson knelt down beside her, tears smarting his eyes.

That asshole had hurt her. Beaten her. Tried to strangle her, judging from the bruises around the tender skin of her neck.

He sheathed his knife and gently reached out to touch her, afraid even the brush of his fingers across her skin would hurt her more.

"Taryn, sweetheart," he said, his voice catching.

"Jackson," she croaked, barely able to speak.

"Shhh, I'm here, baby. I'm here." He lightly palmed her head with his large hand, frustrated he couldn't even see the extent of her injuries. She was whimpering in pain, and he was afraid to even hold her.

The police officer was talking again into his radio as Clarissa started to cry behind them. He heard Blake murmuring to her, guiding her a few feet away from where Taryn lay hurt on the ground.

"What happened?" he asked softly, already knowing the answer.

"Austin," she managed to say. "It was Austin." And then Jackson helplessly watched as her eyes rolled to the back of her head, and she passed out.

Chapter 15

Jackson cursed as the team convened on base the following morning. Clarissa had offered to stay at the hospital with Taryn, and after a quick debrief, he had permission from their commander to head back there. The team would handle the other meetings, but he needed to be at his girl's side.

"How is she?" Blake asked in a clipped tone as they walked toward the bullpen. He had dark circles under his eyes, and Jackson knew he hadn't slept well the night before either.

"Four broken ribs, a fractured eye socket, and swelling in her neck. It's hard for her to talk or eat. She was scared out of her mind when she woke up in the hospital. Luckily, I was there with her. They let me spend the night, and I headed here as soon as Clarissa arrived this morning."

"She'll be okay," Blake said. "She's a fighter."

Jackson clenched his jaw. "She will be, but that

doesn't make it hurt any less to know what she went through. What if we'd gotten back the day before? Or a few hours earlier? She could've been fine."

"Or he could've seen you and shot her immediately," Blake said calmly. "Didn't he have a gun?"

"Fucking hell. I don't even want to think about that," Jackson said.

"As bad as it was, she's alive. She'll recover. And right now, that's what you have to focus on."

Jackson scrubbed his hand across his jaw, frowning. It was true—the situation could've been even worse. He could've shown up and found her dead body there. His stomach roiled even imagining it. No woman should've had to endure what she did. The police figured he'd planned to rape her as well but had been spooked off by neighbors arriving home.

"Austin hasn't been caught yet," Jackson said in a low voice. "The police put out a BOLO for him, and he can't very well go back home. His career as a police officer is over. I'm worried he'll find out she's alive though and come back to finish the job."

"She can stay with us," Blake said.

"Like hell. I'll bring her back to my place. You live right next door. If Austin comes back looking for her, she'd be right there."

Blake nodded, and they entered the room, gathering with the rest of the team.

"How is she?" Ethan asked.

Jackson explained to the others what he'd just told Blake.

"God damn it," Troy said. "Let's go find this asshole right now. He doesn't get away with hurting one of our own."

"You think I don't want to?" Jackson asked. "I've been with Taryn all night. I'm headed back to the hospital as soon as the debrief is over."

"What did the police say?" Logan asked, crossing his arms.

"They've alerted the airports. He flew in yesterday morning but won't be able to leave by commercial airline. That asshole was using his real name. He could've rented a car and driven back."

"He's got connections though," Ethan pressed. "What if he had a fake ID? Then couldn't he catch a flight?"

"They have his picture," Logan pressed. "He's probably still around here lying low."

"Hailey was so worried about her," Grayson said. "The women were all supposed to meet up last night. Hailey got stuck late at work and hadn't made it over yet. She found out about Taryn at the same time that I did."

"I'm glad the other women are okay," Jackson said, looking around at his teammates. "It doesn't make seeing Taryn any easier though. She'll be even more terrified now."

"It's almost over," Blake assured him. "The police will find Austin, and he'll be arrested and locked up. Taryn won't have to look over her shoulder anymore. It fucking sucks that she went through that, but now we all know his name and what he looks like. The police already have a report on him."

Jackson heaved out a sigh. "True. She won't necessarily have to report him for his abusive behavior in the past. I know she didn't want to relive any of that."

The men all looked up as their commander stormed into the room. He looked madder than hell, and Jackson raised his eyebrows. "I've been dealing with an issue regarding one of the other SEAL teams," he muttered. "How's Taryn?" he asked, eyeing Jackson.

"Recovering. She'll be okay."

Their CO nodded. "Then let's get down to business. We'll debrief over the op in Algeria and discuss a few other situations unfolding."

The team exchanged glances with one another.

"A new leader has already taken over in Afghanistan for Sayed."

"No surprise," Troy muttered. "Those terrorist groups are like a bunch of cockroaches. You crush one and a hundred others are scuttling around."

Their CO's lips quirked. "Affirmative, but this one is personal. There's been video footage of the two missing Americans."

"They're still alive," Ethan said, pounding his fist on the table. "Then let's fucking move in."

"Easy Everglades," Blake cautioned.

"It hasn't been broadcast over the media yet, but we intercepted the communication. They're alive and planning to show the video footage of the two women soon."

"And their condition?"

Their commander eyed Ethan. "They were sitting up and able to talk."

He nodded, relaxing his stance slightly.

"Are we going to go over the Algeria op?" Jackson asked, suddenly feeling impatient. He didn't like the fact that two women were being held hostage any more than the rest of them, but it sounded like they still didn't have a location.

The CO met Jackson's gaze. "Go back to the hospital, K-Bar. I'll get your After-Action Review later. The other men can fill me in for now."

Jackson jumped up so fast, his chair fell over. "Thank you, sir," he said as Blake leaned over to right it. Jackson was already moving out the door, ready to rush back to the hospital. He needed to be with Taryn. Nothing else mattered at the moment.

***

Taryn smiled as Jackson walked into her hospital room. For a moment, she thought she was dreaming, but no, he was really here. He had dark circles under his eyes and was in his camo uniform. She wasn't sure what time it was and if he'd stopped here on his way to or from work. She'd dreamt he'd been with her last night, but when she awoke, Clarissa had been asleep on the chair in her hospital room.

But now it really was him, and relief flooded through her.

"Hi sweetheart," he said, crossing over to her hospital bed. "I had to go into base for an hour or so, but my CO sent me here." He set a cup of water down on the table beside her. "I just told Clarissa to head home."

"How long have I been here?" she croaked as he sank into the chair beside her bed.

Jackson helped her to take a sip of the water, and she didn't miss the look on his face as she grimaced in pain. It hurt to move and even to swallow. Jackson looked like he was in pain himself watching her hurting. It was caring and sweet, and once again, she could hardly imagine why this amazing man was so worried about her.

He helped her get settled back into her bed again, nothing but gentle with her despite his strength.

"Jackson?" she asked when he hadn't answered her.

"Shhh," he said, running a hand over her hair. His dark eyes met hers, and she could see the concern and love in them. He hovered at her bedside like she was the most important thing in the world to him. Her. A woman who'd just been beaten and nearly killed by her crazed ex-husband.

Jackson cleared his throat, seemingly needing to pull himself together before answering.

"Just one night. I got home with the team yesterday and headed straight to see you. Clarissa was outside your townhouse with a police officer and—"

He cut off as tears filled her eyes.

"It killed me to find you like that," he said in a choked voice. "When I saw your body lying there, I thought—" He lifted a hand to his face, unable to even finish.

"Thank you," she whispered.

He shook his head, looking near tears himself, then leaned over and lightly kissed her forehead. "You don't have to thank me. I didn't do a fucking thing. I'm pissed as hell that asshole wasn't still there when I showed up. I would've beaten him to a pulp and then killed him myself for daring to touch you."

"What happened to him?" she managed to ask.

Jackson got her another sip of water, running his hand over her head again.

"It sounds like you'll be here for a couple of days, but I want you to come stay with me after you're released. Austin hasn't been caught yet."

Her eyes widened.

"The police have a BOLO out on him, and the guys are going to do some searching on their own later after they're done with their briefings. Blake's house has one of those doorbell cameras. I wish we'd have gotten one set up for you—then we might've had an even clearer picture. They have the car he was driving and are trying to enhance the images to get the license plates."

"He's still here," she croaked.

"It's possible. We have a couple of days off since we just got back. I'll be with you, but the other guys will be looking for him. We've got the model of the car he rented, and we'll be checking the nearby hotels."

"What if he comes here?" she asked, suddenly feeling frightened. She'd been in a light sleep before Jackson had walked in. What if Austin came back to finish the job?

"The hospital has security and has been informed of your situation. There's a police officer stationed in the hallway right now."

"Good."

"They think Austin got spooked off yesterday when one of your neighbors got home."

Tears filled her eyes. He'd pushed her to the ground and hit and hurt her. She hadn't been raped, as far as she could tell. She wasn't sore there, and certainly they would have told her that, wouldn't they? She remembered him choking her and then everything went black.

"He'll come back looking for me."

Jackson nodded. "There's a chance of that. A

damn good possibility considering he tracked you down and came all the way across the country. I'll be here at your side in the hospital. That asshole is crazy."

"My whole body hurts," she said.

Jackson reached out and gently took her hand, his other remaining on her head. "I hate that he hurt you—that he even touched you. I'm going to find him, and I swear to God, Taryn, you'll never have to worry about him again."

She squeezed her eyes shut as a few tears formed.

"What's wrong? Should I call the nurse?"

"I don't want you to risk your job for me. You can't chase after Austin."

"Shhh," he murmured. "Don't talk too much and hurt your throat more. You let me worry about that. I'll make sure that you're safe and that he can't ever touch you again."

Her tears did fall then, and Jackson looked almost helpless as he sat at her side. She was so thankful he was there, but it hurt with every word that she uttered. She'd talk to him more when she had recovered. She'd tell him how much he meant to her and how she didn't want to live without him.

But at the moment?

She just wanted to sleep, with the man she was falling in love with right there at her side.

Chapter 16

Two days later, Jackson helped Taryn up the steps of her townhouse. He'd wanted to bring her back to his apartment, but she'd insisted that he take her home. And stay with her, of course. Blake had agreed that it was safer since he was right next door.

Jackson hadn't wanted to take Taryn back to the place where Austin had attacked her, but when she'd teared up saying she wanted her own room and bed, he hadn't been able to deny her anything. He'd ordered a ton of groceries since he'd be staying there, too, and the team had cleaned up her backyard while she'd been in the hospital.

It might've been fall, but they'd laid sod down, trimmed the bushes, and planted some seasonal flowers. Clarissa and Blake had even hung a hammock up under the deck. Now when Taryn went back there, hopefully she wouldn't be immediately reminded of Austin. Jackson knew it would take time, but he hoped to eventually persuade her to spend some time in the backyard with him. He wanted good memories to take away the bad.

He'd bought a grill for her deck, insisting that he'd be doing a lot of the cooking since he was staying with her.

They hadn't discussed exactly how long that would be, but Jackson had brought over a suitcase and duffle bag full of things. He wasn't planning to leave anytime soon—not as long as Taryn wanted him there.

And who was he kidding?

Her townhouse was a hell of a lot more spacious than his apartment. He wouldn't mind living there with her permanently, not that they'd specifically discussed it.

He certainly didn't want her out of his life now, and she'd been so happy she'd cried when he said they could stay at her place instead of his.

"How are you feeling?" he asked later that night.

"Tired. Sore. But better than a couple of days ago. Do you have work tomorrow?"

Jackson shook his head no. "The rest of the team is, but I was able to get a few more days off. I might go run early in the morning, but Raptor and Clarissa said they'd come hang out here with you before he heads to PT with the rest of the guys."

"Okay," she said. "You won't get in trouble or anything for missing it?"

"No, sweetheart. I arranged for a few extra days to be here with you."

"Okay," she said again, smiling. For how shy and hesitant she'd been before his mission, Taryn seemed more confident of herself now. It was strange. He'd figured she'd be even more terrified after Austin had attacked her, but maybe, deep down, she realized that it was almost over. He'd be caught, and she'd be safe. She wouldn't need to look over her shoulder forever. And Jackson wasn't about to leave her side. The police had gotten a couple of tips, and he hoped the asshole would be in jail before the weekend.

"I thought I could grill some steaks later on," he said as he carried Taryn's small bag of belongings into her bedroom. He'd brought a few things to her while she was in the hospital, and now they were already back at her house. Taryn had a small, queen-sized bed, which made him smirk. He was a big guy, and if he did end up staying here longer, they'd have to see about getting a larger bed for them. At the moment, nothing sounded better than curling up with Taryn in his arms though. He wouldn't mind having to hold her close. Not at all.

"I don't have a grill," she said, pulling some clean clothes out of her dresser. The moment they'd gotten home from the hospital, she'd said she wanted to shower and change. He had his own bags to carry up, so he'd leave her to it while he unpacked a few of his things and made sure the groceries he'd ordered had arrived.

"I bought one," he said with a shrug. "I figured I'd be staying here a while. Logan and Ethan picked it up for me yesterday—Logan's got a pick-up truck. They even set it up for us, so we're good to go."

"Wow. Well okay then."

"You're not going to protest?" he teased, raising his eyebrows.

"I'm done fighting this—us. When you left on your mission, I realized how much I wanted to make this work. How I hadn't told you that I was falling for you. I know I wanted to take things slow, but Jackson, I just want you."

Jackson nodded, watching her closely. He wanted to pull her into his arms, kiss her, and then take her to bed and hold her tight. He knew she wanted to clean up though. And he wasn't about to make love to her while she was recovering. "It makes me happy as hell for you to say that, sweetheart. Go shower and change. I'll unpack a few things and be here when you're done."

He carried his suitcase and duffle bag upstairs from her living room, listening to the sound of the shower still coming from the bathroom. Hell, she could stay in there for hours if she wanted. As long as she was happy and safe.

Taryn didn't have many clothes here, which made him frown, but it did make unpacking easier. She'd given him an entire side of the dresser. He'd planned to be here for at least a few weeks while she healed from her injuries, but he wouldn't complain if he never left.

Almost losing her made Jackson realize even more how much he needed her in his life. He'd go at whatever pace she wanted, but hell. He wasn't about to let the best thing in his life slip away.

His mouth dropped open a moment later when Taryn emerged from the bathroom wearing only a silky, floral robe. He knew she'd carried clean clothes in there, but she'd elected to come out in only this, knowing Jackson was here in her bedroom.

Taryn's hair was damp, hanging down to her shoulders, and he could still see the faint hint of bruising around her neck and near her eye. She was the most beautiful woman he'd ever seen though, and his cock stirred just looking at her.

It was wrong to even think that. She was injured. She needed him to hold her, not pull her to bed and make love to her for hours.

"I was going to get dressed but thought you could just hold me for a while."

He nodded, his gaze raking over her beautiful body. She'd put on her rose-scented lotion and was so soft and sweet to look at, it practically hurt.

"Come here, sweetheart," he said, his voice gravel.

She walked toward him, resting her hands on his chest, then stood up on her tiptoes to kiss him. He'd kissed her briefly before when they'd first gotten home, but that had been chaste and sweet. This kiss was an explosion. She might still be hurting and sore, but she kissed him hard enough to let him know that she was claiming him as hers. It was erotic and arousing as hell having her make a move like that. Taryn had been hesitant before, but now she wanted him. And Jackson felt about ten feet tall.

His arms wrapped around her as his mouth met with hers, and then he was lifting her up, carrying her to bed.

"I want you to make love to me," she said, looking like a goddess spread out before him after he'd laid her down.

"You're hurt," he said gently.

"You'll be careful. I thought I'd never see you again—that Austin would kill me, and I'd never have a chance to tell you I was falling in love with you. I need you, Jackson."

He ducked down, his arms caging her in, and kissed her harder then. She tasted sweet, like strawberries and cream, and she smelled of roses. His erection was painful against the confines of his pants, but this was about her. Her comfort. Her pleasure.

"Let me take care of you," he murmured, softly kissing his way down her neck. She shuddered beneath him, and he undid the tie of her robe, baring her to him. Her breasts were full and gorgeous, with pale nipples that he longed to tongue and suck. He lightly ran his hand over her breasts, loving how she arched into his touch. Unable to resist, his mouth followed. He licked one gorgeous nipple, then sucked it into his mouth, feasting on Taryn as she clutched his head and whimpered.

"Jackson, oh God."

He lightly flickered his tongue over her nipple, loving as she writhed beneath him. "I'll take care of you, Taryn," he said, his voice gruff. "I'll give you everything." He shifted to her other breast, laving the same attention on it. Her full globes were a handful, and he squeezed one, loving the eroticism of his muscular hand on her bare breast.

She watched him, seemingly as entranced as he was. Jackson softened his touch, caressing one breast gently while he kissed and sucked on the other one.

Taryn gasped, arching up toward him, and he could smell her arousal. He licked his way around her nipple, enjoying every pant and moan that she made. He could feast on her breasts for hours, but he was anxious to pleasure her. To taste her sweet folds and make her shatter apart in his arms.

Softly, he kissed his way down her stomach. She was a little too thin from those weeks of barely eating, but he'd do what he could to make sure she was healthy and strong.

"You're beautiful," he breathed reverently.

"I'm nervous."

"I'll never hurt you, sweetheart. Let me love you."

She shivered as he kissed his way lower toward her sex, and then he was eagerly lying in front of her, ready to give Taryn everything.

***

"You smell so good," Jackson growled, kissing her swollen sex.

She trembled before him, both nervous and excited. She'd never felt as turned-on as she did in this moment, and she knew it was purely Jackson who caused her to feel this way. His touch. His kisses. His gentleness.

Jackson was everything she'd ever dreamed about in a man, and he was here before her, ready to love on her. His large hands spread her thighs open, and there was something erotic and sinful at having this massive man kneel before her.

"Jackson," she breathed, flushing in both arousal and embarrassment. "I—I've never done this."

He growled in approval. "It's true," he said, lightly nuzzling his cheek against her. His whiskers abraded her nether lips, and she shook. "You smell fucking amazing. I'm honored to be the first man who's gone down on you. The only man," he said, his voice gravel.

"Please Jackson," she whispered.

He hitched her legs over his wide shoulders, and she practically panted as she lay spread out before him on her bed. She was at his complete and utter mercy, but instead of being frightened, she was completely aroused.

He lightly ran his tongue up her slit, finally trailing it through her arousal-drenched folds.

"Jesus," he growled. "You taste so sweet; I'll never get enough. I can't get over how wet you are for me." He lightly ran his thick fingers through her folds, seemingly in awe. She blushed furiously, watching in amazement as he lifted both fingers to his mouth, sucking off her arousal.

"Mine," he said.

That was all the warning she had before he ducked down again and pleasured her, licking and sucking and kissing until she was bucking up off the bed. His tongue trailed through her folds, knowing exactly how to tease her.

She'd never had a man make her feel this way before. Never. And it was purely sinful what this man could do with his mouth.

Sparks of desire shot through her, and she moaned—actually moaned—at how good it felt. One thick finger slid to her center, and then he was easing inside, stretching her inner walls. He added a second finger, and she gasped.

"Jackson, oh my God!"

What would it feel like having his cock thrusting into her? His fingers were magical enough. She could barely imagine what he could do with his dick. Jackson looked up, watching her, as his fingers thrust in and out, his thumb rubbing over her clit.

"Oh God, oh God!" she pleaded.

She was too far gone to feel embarrassed anymore. Jackson touching her made her want to explode. The pressure was building, and it was so much, so fast, she swore she began to see stars.

Jackson lowered his wicked mouth and latched onto her clit, sucking her tender bud into his mouth as he drove her higher. His lips and tongue worked their magic, and she finally screamed out her release, helpless to the man before her.

It could've been minutes or hours before she finally came back to her senses. Jackson was still nuzzling her gently, slowly bringing her back down. Her legs were over his wide shoulders, and his eyes heated as he gazed at her core.

He pulled his fingers out, sucking off her juices as she blushed.

"Jackson, make love to me," she said, watching as his eyes widened with arousal.

"You're injured." His voice was strained, and she knew he had to be ready. He was more concerned about her than his own pleasure.

"I need you," she pleaded.

He slowly eased her legs off his shoulders and stood, quickly removing his shirt and pants. Jackson was a sight to behold, with broad pecs and an abdomen she wanted to sit up and lick if she weren't still sore from her injuries. As he shoved his boxers down, his cock sprung out, hard, thick, and ready. It bobbed as he pulled his wallet from his pants, producing a condom. He sheathed himself and then gently moved her toward the edge of her bed.

"When you're better, I can't wait to cover you with my body. To feel you beneath me. I'll be gentle tonight though, sweetheart."

He lifted her legs, wrapping them around his waist as he edged closer to her. His cock brushed against her still sensitive clit, and she gasped. "You're mine, sweetheart," he murmured before lining himself up and gently nudging inside.

Jackson went slow—so very slow. He was big, but she was wet and ready for him thanks to that mind-blowing orgasm. "God, you're tight," he muttered. "You feel amazing."

"Keep going," she urged. "I want all of you."

Jackson inched in further, and she gasped, her hands flying to her breasts. It felt so good having Jackson inside her, like he was made for her alone. Sex had never felt like this before—never. Their gazes locked and then Jackson's raked down her body, taking in her breasts, her stomach, and finally, where their sexes joined.

"You're beautiful," he ground out.

"So are you," she gasped, looking at the wall of muscle and man before her. His muscular arms held her legs, and she was spread out before him waiting to be claimed. She wanted this. Wanted him. "Take me," she pleaded.

"I'll go slow," he said again, seemingly more to himself than her. And Jackson began thrusting, watching her face for her reaction. Her ribs did still ache, but she didn't care. It would take months to heal from multiple broken bones. She wanted him to make love to her, to make her his. She wanted and needed this.

His thumb slid to her clit, and he strummed it as he slowly made love to her. It was careful and sweet, and she tightened her legs around him. "I love you," he said, his voice gruff. The truth shone in his eyes. Jackson did love her, just as she loved him.

His thrusts increased in speed, despite his trying to hold back. With every stroke he brought her higher, closer. His erection was long and thick, and she couldn't do anything but hold on for the ride as he took her. His thumb swept over her clit again, and she cried out, orgasming a second time as Jackson bucked into her again and stilled, releasing as well.

Moments later, he was crawling into her bed, carefully easing her into his arms.

"That was amazing," she murmured, nuzzling up against him. Her head lay on his broad chest, one of her legs thrown over his muscular thigh. He was solid and strong and real. Safe.

"You're amazing," he said, running a hand over her still-damp hair.

She nodded but yawned sleepily, content to drift off in the safety of Jackson's arms.

Chapter 17

The following week, Jackson returned to work with the rest of his team. There'd been no signs of Austin, but his leave had come to an end, and it was time to get back to his routine. Clarissa had gone to Taryn's for the day, and another guy from base had agreed to hang out with the women. It was unusual, to be certain, but until Austin was caught, Jackson didn't feel comfortable leaving her alone. Taryn could work on a few projects from home, and Clarissa could prepare for her lectures that night.

The police officers had protected Taryn while she was in the hospital, but now that she was back home, it had been entirely on him. Jackson couldn't ask his buddies to be there every day though. He needed to figure out somewhere safe for her to go.

Or track down Austin himself.

The day dragged on, with drills out on the water and more meetings about several situations unfolding around the world. The Pentagon had praised them for bringing the terror cell leader in Algeria to justice. Although most of the world would never know the details of what had transpired, it still filled Jackson with pride to know another job had been well done and another terrorist had been taken out.

Leaving base later than he wanted to, Jackson finally headed home after an exhausting day. He was tired from the grueling training sessions they'd done and was looking forward to relaxing for the evening with his girl.

Jackson decided to stop by the grocery store on the way home to pick up a couple of things. They hadn't gone out over the weekend, preferring instead to stay home while Taryn recovered and make lazy love while they spent hours in bed together.

Taryn was beautiful and sweet. She'd been slightly nervous the first time they'd been together, but the way she'd opened up to him made his heart soar. He was still infinitely gentle, given that she was still recovering, but every time he entered her body, slowly making love and claiming her as his, he fell for her a little bit more.

Jackson slammed the door to his SUV shut, planning to grab just a few items from the store before he went home. He'd texted his buddy to say he'd be there in twenty minutes. He owed his friend big time for spending his entire day off with Taryn, but Jackson knew he'd do the same for any of the men on base if their loved ones were in danger.

He was glancing down at his phone, smiling as he read a text from Taryn, so he didn't immediately notice the car speeding toward him. Another car honked, and then Jackson looked up, diving out of the way as an older model Ford came racing his way.

The car slammed into another parked vehicle, and Jackson didn't need to look at the driver as he jumped out to know it was Austin.

He'd already dialed 911 as the crazed man stumbled out and came toward him, weapon in hand.

"911, what's your emergency?"

"My girlfriend was attacked last week by her ex-husband. He's here now at the Supermart, holding a gun and threatening me. There's a BOLO out for his arrest. Austin Brown."

Jackson hung up before the dispatcher could ask for more information. Other people were now calling it in as well, running and hiding from the crazy guy who was wielding a gun.

"You stole her from me, jackass!" Austin yelled, stumbling slightly as he took a step toward Jackson. "You thought you could fucking take what was mine? She's my wife!" he screamed. He fired a shot into the air as people gasped and ducked behind their cars. A child began crying, and out of the corner of his eye, Jackson saw a mom pushing her two children to the ground.

Austin smashed the window of the rental car he'd been driving, screaming obscenities.

"He's got a gun!" someone yelled.

"Shots fired! Shots fired!"

"Help!" a woman screamed.

Austin fired into the air once more and then aimed the gun directly at Jackson's chest as he stood there. He could run and take cover, but he didn't want any civilians to be harmed. Austin had already fired his weapon twice. And this was between him and Austin.

He wouldn't cower and hide while innocent

women and children were hurt.

"She left you," Jackson said, taking a step toward the madman. "She divorced you and fled. Get the hell out of here."

Sirens sounded in the distance, but Jackson's vision was focused entirely on Austin. His hand shook as he held the gun, and Jackson tried to gauge the likelihood of tackling him without harm coming to anyone else. He held his hand up, hoping to slow Austin's advance.

"Fuck you!" Austin screamed.

"Slow your roll. She left you, and it's over. Why don't you turn around and head home? There's nothing left for you here."

"Head home? My life is over! My career is ruined. And it's all because of that bitch!"

A baby started screaming, and Austin looked around, growing more agitated. The gun shook in his hands, and Jackson didn't hesitate. He reached around his back to the K-Bar knife he carried and pulled it free from its sheath.

"Shut up, just shut up!" Austin screamed.

He looked back at Jackson, raising the gun again, but he was too slow. Jackson threw the knife at Austin just as he pulled the trigger. Jackson dove to the side, and the knife landed in Austin's chest as the bullet pierced the windshield of another car. Blood pooled from Austin's knife wound, and he slumped to the ground, dropping the gun.

Jackson sprung up and ran over, kicking the gun away as several people screamed, but Austin was already dead, his eyes rolling to the back of his head. Jackson stared at him a beat, feeling no remorse for killing the man who'd hurt Taryn over and over again.

Who'd thought nothing of shooting at him, risking the lives of innocents all around them.

Three police cars came racing into the parking lot, the officers jumping out as Jackson held up his hands and stepped back. They climbed out of their vehicles, guns drawn and pointed at Austin, but it was over. Taryn's ex-husband was dead, and she was finally really and truly free.

Epilogue

Taryn beamed as the doorbell rang, and Jackson poked his head in the sliding glass doors from where he stood on the deck grilling.

"You got it?" he asked, his dark gaze meeting hers.

"Yep, I'm good, baby," she said with a smile. She practically skipped downstairs to let in Clarissa and Blake and was surprised to see Logan and his date already there as well.

"We heard there was a party," Blake quipped, carrying in two six-packs of beer as Clarissa held up a huge platter of ribs to stick on the grill.

"Sorry, I couldn't resist," she said with a grin. "I'm a Texas girl at heart!"

"We brought beer and wine," Logan said, holding up both as his date snuggled up to him.

"Yo, Raptor and Hurricane!" Troy whooped, grinning from ear-to-ear as he hurried up the steps with a pretty blonde. She was a different woman than the date he'd been with a month ago, Taryn noticed. Apparently, some things never changed with these guys. Half the team seemed to have a new woman with them every week.

"Come in," Taryn said, smiling at her friends. Her friends. Because they really were now. The entire team had welcomed her as one of their own, and she knew how lucky she was to have real friends. "Jackson's grilling out on the deck."

The group began walking upstairs when the doorbell rang yet again. "At least everyone's punctual," Clarissa said with a laugh. "I'll go give the food to Jackson."

"I got the door," Troy said. He turned around and opened it, and Taryn saw Hailey and Grayson standing there.

She waved at them both but continued up the stairs as the small foyer and stairway were already getting crowded. Jackson came walking in, grinning, and he ducked down for a quick kiss. She practically shivered as his hand rested on the small of her back, pulling her close.

Her ribs had completely healed now, and she and Jackson had spent the morning making love. She'd sat astride him, her legs spread wide as she rode his cock. One of his hands had gripped her hip, steadying her, the other at the small of her back, just as it was now.

Jackson winked, knowing she was thinking the same thing that he was. He ducked down, his lips at her ear. "Tonight, sweetheart," he promised. "We'll do it all over again."

Troy chuckled as he watched them. "Hey K-Bar, get a room," he joked. His date giggled and lightly swatted at him. He grinned even wider and pulled her into his arms for a searing kiss.

Blake popped the top of a beer bottle and looked around at the group that had already assembled. "I can't believe we're already having another celebration. K-Bar has officially moved in with Taryn. She must be a saint for being willing to put up with him—"

"Boo!" Logan interjected loudly as the others laughed.

"She's damn lucky to have you," Blake said with a grin.

"Amen to that," Jackson said, grabbing his own longneck and toasting his SEAL team leader. "And I'm lucky as hell to have her."

"And I'm thrilled you're staying here," Clarissa said. "It wouldn't have been the same if you moved in with Jackson."

"Who wants a margarita?" Hailey asked. "Ladies? We never did get to have our girls' night."

The group moved around the kitchen, grabbing drinks and appetizers for themselves as Jackson and some of the guys headed out to the deck to start grilling. The doorbell rang again, and Taryn excused herself, hurrying downstairs.

Ethan was frowning as she opened the door.

"Hi. Is everything okay?" she asked.

He shook his head. "We might be headed out tomorrow. Shit. Jackson will be pissed I just told you that. This is supposed to be a celebration."

"Come on in," she said, shutting the door behind him. "What happened? I mean, I know you can't really tell me, but you look upset."

"You remember Hailey's friend?"

Taryn nodded. "The one who was missing."

"They found her."

Taryn gasped as Ethan excused himself, jogging up the steps to talk to his teammates. By the time she'd locked the door and headed upstairs, she saw all of the guys glancing down at their cell phones.

Jackson moved toward her, his eyes worried. "Hell, sweetheart. This is supposed to be a party, but the guys and I have to leave tomorrow."

"Ethan just told me."

"Fuck," he muttered.

Taryn reached up, putting her hand on his cheek. "It's okay, baby. This is nothing like your last op. Austin is dead, remember? I'll be fine when you're gone."

He swallowed and nodded. "I know. I just hate to leave you."

"You'll do your job," she assured him. "What if it was me that had been kidnapped?"

"I'd search the ends of the earth to find you."

Taryn nodded. "And you'll find Hailey's friend."

"Hell, I love you," Jackson said, ducking down for a kiss. The others were talking around them, discussing the pending op and the need to cut the night short after they ate. Normally the women would never know about their mission and where they were headed, but this was personal. And Hailey would've found out at work anyway. Nothing about the situation was normal.

At the moment, it didn't matter though. Taryn knew Jackson would be safe as he rushed off to save the world once again. He'd saved her more than once, first as she'd struggled just to get by and then from her crazy ex-husband. She knew her life would never be the same because of him, and she couldn't be happier.

"I love you, too," she whispered.

And then Jackson kissed her again, passionately, deeply, their bodies pressed together, until the only thing that mattered was that moment and the two of them. Forever.

About the Author

USA Today Bestselling Author Makenna Jameison writes sizzling romantic suspense, including the addictive Alpha SEALs series.

Makenna loves the beach, strong coffee, red wine, and traveling. She lives in Washington DC with her husband and two daughters.

Visit www.makennajameison.com to discover your next great read.

Made in the USA
Middletown, DE
22 September 2022